SOPHIE'S FRIEND IN NEED

ALSO BY NORMA CHARLES

All the Way to Mexico (2003)
Fuzzy Wuzzy (2002)
Criss Cross, Double Cross:
Sophie Alias Star Girl to the Rescue (2002)
The Accomplice (2001)
Sophie Sea to Sea: Star Girl's Cross-Canada Adventures (1999)
Runaway (1999)
Dolphin Alert! (1998)

SOPHIE'S FRIEND IN NEED

Further Adventures of Sophie Alias Star Girl

NORMA CHARLES

An imprint of
Beach Holme Publishing
Vancouver

First Edition

This book is published by Beach Holme Publishing, Suite 1010, 409 Granville Street, Vancouver, B.C. V6C 1T2. *www.beachholme.bc.ca*. This is a Sandcastle Book.

The publisher gratefully acknowledges the financial support of the Canada Council for the Arts and of the British Columbia Arts Council. The publisher also acknowledges the financial assistance received from the Government of Canada through the Book Publishing Industry Development Program (BPIDP) for its publishing activities.

The Canada Council | Le Conseil des Arts
for the Arts | du Canada

BRITISH
COLUMBIA
ARTS COUNCIL
Supported by the Province of British Columbia

Editor: Suzanne Norman
Production and Design: Jen Hamilton
Cover Art: Susan Reilly
Author Photograph: Brian Wood

Printed and bound in Canada by AGMV Marquis Imprimeur

Library and Archives Canada Cataloguing in Publication

Charles, Norma M.
     Sophie's friend in need : further adventures of Sophie alias Star Girl/Norma Charles.

"A Sandcastle book."
ISBN 0-88878-449-X

    I. Title.

PS8555.H4224S674 2004   jC813'.54   C2004-905200-4

For my grandchildren, Clarissa and Tarin,
whom I don't see often enough

ACKNOWLEDGEMENTS

I am grateful for the help of my writing friends and colleagues who offered wise advice about this manuscript in progress, especially James Heneghan, Irene Watts, Ellen Schwartz, Kathleen Waldron, Linda Bailey, Joan Weir, and Ann Walsh.

I would also like to thank everyone at Beach Holme Publishing for continuing to be enthusiastic Sophie fans, with particular thanks to publisher Michael Carroll and editor Suzanne Norman for their insightful editing.

ONE

The *Seabird* skimmed over the sparkling sea of British Columbia's Howe Sound like a bird in flight. At least that was what the motorboat should have been doing. But with a load of twenty chattering girls, two young women counsellors, and camp supplies for a week, it was too heavy to skim. So it furrowed through the waves like a farmer's plough, spraying salt water into the young campers' faces.

Three girls shivered at the front of the boat and pulled up the blue canvas tarp as shelter. The tarp smelled dank and musty, but Sophie LaGrange didn't care. She was much too excited. Camping! They were on their way to Latona Camp on Gambier Island for a whole week. It was summer 1950, Sophie was eleven years old, and it was the first time in her entire life that she would be away from her family.

She was sitting between her friend, Elizabeth Proctor, and another girl, who was buried in an oversize yellow raincoat. The

1

girl hadn't acknowledged Sophie's presence, and she didn't know the stranger's name yet. When they first climbed aboard the *Seabird*, Sophie had said hi to the girl, but she had only nodded slightly without even glancing her way. She was a skinny, grey sort of person with pale straight hair, a pale ashy face, and pale grey eyes.

Sophie bounced and wiggled in her seat. Soon, soon, they would be at camp! She glanced back at Porteau Cove where Papa had dropped Elizabeth and her off that morning, after a two-hour drive from their homes in Maillardville. They had travelled through New Westminster, then all along Kingsway in Burnaby, right through Vancouver and across the Lions Gate Bridge, and all through West Vancouver to Horseshoe Bay. Then they'd driven along a steep gravel mountain road at the edge of the sea. Sophie had thought they'd never get to Porteau Cove, but they finally did.

Two Latona Camp counsellors had met them at the dock. After giving Papa a quick goodbye hug, Sophie had excitedly climbed aboard the *Seabird* with Elizabeth and they had grabbed the front seat.

"I can hardly see the dock at Porteau Cove now, can you?" Sophie now asked Elizabeth, staring back to where the dock blended into the surrounding foliage, beach, and water.

Elizabeth looked, too, then shook her head. "Where's that island? When are we going to get there?" she muttered, her voice tight with worry.

"Papa said it would take only half an hour, so we should be there soon. I bet that's Gambier straight ahead."

A green island shaped like a broad haystack with steep, rounded sides and a bumpy top was taking form in the light mist.

"I hope they don't make us pray all day long at that camp," Elizabeth said.

"I'm sure they won't. Maman said that even though it's run by Catholic Charities, kids from all different churches will be there."

Elizabeth seemed bleak. She blinked hard.

Sophie patted her arm. "Your mom's going to be fine, Liz. You know when my oldest brother, Joseph, had his appendix out, he was outside playing baseball with his friends the next week."

Elizabeth rubbed her nose on the back of her hand and sniffed. She nodded. "That's what my dad said. He said Mom might even be out of the hospital when we get back from camp."

A big wave crashed against the boat, and cold water suddenly sprayed into their faces as if a garden hose had been turned on full blast.

Elizabeth shrieked and ducked under the tarp. "What if this boat flips right over and we all fall out and drown!" she cried, trying to hold back her hair and red ribbon as the wind whipped them around her face.

"Don't worry," Sophie said, scrunching up her eyes as more spray splashed over the bow. "We won't flip over and we won't fall out. Even if we did, we've got these life preservers tied on, so we wouldn't sink."

Her hero, Star Girl, would never be scared about a little spraying water. Sophie worked her hand under her life preserver and into her jacket pocket, searching for her Star Girl Super Bounce Ball. She squeezed it. Months ago she had sent away for the ball using a form at the back of a Star Girl comic book. She had played with it so much that it wasn't as shiny and red as it used to be. As long as she had her Star Girl ball, she wasn't afraid of anything.

"But I can't swim very well," Elizabeth whined. "I'd probably drown in a second in all that water. I knew I should never have come."

"We'll have lots of fun at camp. And it doesn't matter if you can't swim that great. Like I said, these will keep us afloat."

Sophie cheerfully patted her bulky orange life preserver.

"Oh, no!" Elizabeth squealed. "Look, mine's come undone!"

"Here, I'll tie it up for you." Sophie pushed her Star Girl ball deep into her pocket, then tied the long beige straps on Elizabeth's life preserver into a tight bow. "There. Tight as can be."

"The water's so deep here." Elizabeth peered over the side, her eyes widening. She stared at the waves cresting and splashing against the hull. "I bet it's a mile deep at least. And I bet there are sharks and even giant octopuses in the water."

Sophie shook her head. "I'm sure there are no sharks around here. Right?" she asked the silent girl sitting next to her.

Frowning, the girl pulled the hood of her raincoat lower over her eyes and turned away.

"How come she's so mad at me?" Sophie whispered in Elizabeth's ear. "What did I do to her?"

Elizabeth shrugged. "She's just rude," she whispered back, wrinkling her nose as if the grey girl smelled. She pointed at the stranger's feet and giggled. The girl was wearing shiny white patent leather shoes with straps. The toes were scuffed and dirty.

Not exactly the best footwear for camping, Sophie thought. She couldn't help giggling, too, as she admired her own brand-new navy running shoes that her mother had bought at Eaton's especially for camp.

Elizabeth sighed. "I'll be so glad when we finally get onto dry land again."

The mist had evaporated, and the island loomed in the distance.

"Hey, look!" Sophie said. "You can already see the trees on the island. And look at all those high cliffs."

As the *Seabird* drew nearer to the island, its motor slowed to a putter to avoid the jagged reefs and islets strewn with seaweed and bits of driftwood that rocked in the boat's wake. A flock of gulls took flight and screeched at them, wheeling around on outstretched wings. The sea glistened as if it were covered with thousands of sequins. The boat rounded a point of land, and a collection of weathered wooden buildings nestled among tall evergreen trees at the edge of a horseshoe-shape bay came into view.

"There's the camp!" Sophie shouted, excitement bubbling in her stomach.

"Finally," Elizabeth muttered.

A sloping ramp connected the island to a long floating dock beside a rocky beach. At the top of the ramp a Union Jack on a pole flapped a friendly welcome.

"What's that big log building with all the windows?" Elizabeth wondered aloud. "Do you think that's where we sleep?"

"I don't know," Sophie said. "Could be. Or maybe we'll be staying in one of the smaller cabins behind it."

"They wouldn't expect us to stay in those old dingy things. They're not even painted." Elizabeth sniffed and patted her hair ribbon.

As they approached the dock, the sound of the motor faded away and the boat bobbed gently against the dockside.

"We're here! Finally we're here!" Sophie quivered with anticipation. She licked her salty lips, eased her Star Girl ball out of her pocket again, held it in her palm, and gave it an extra squeeze.

"Everyone remain seated, please," one of the counsellors directed from the back of the boat.

The counsellor's name was Miss Rosy. The woman looked like a jolly sort of person. She was plump and had a mass of curly blond hair, pink cheeks, and an infectious grin.

"Now, I'll just mosey on up to the bow and tie us to the dock. Then you girls will be able to get out. Don't move yet. Excuse me, excuse me," the young woman said as she made her way to the front, pushing past the rows of girls. "Sorry," she grunted as she bumped between Sophie and the silent grey girl.

Miss Rosy clambered onto the bow on her hands and knees and grasped the rope that was tied there. As she reached out for the edge of the dock, the boat lurched and bounced. Suddenly, with a surprised scream and a big splash, Miss Rosy fell in headfirst!

Sophie gasped. A Star Girl rescue flashed through her mind. She leaped onto the bow and peered over the side.

"Watch out, Sophie!" Elizabeth cried. "You'll fall in, too!"

The boat jerked again, and Sophie lost her balance. She clutched at the bow but missed. The next thing she knew she was tumbling into the water, as well.

Her breath caught in her throat as the cold water closed over her head, filling her ears, eyes, and nose. She flailed her arms and kicked her feet until she bobbed to the surface. Blinking hard and sputtering, she coughed up the salty water and strained against the bulky life preserver tight around her ears and neck.

Miss Rosy was thrashing around, too, her life preserver pushing up her chin. "Help!" she burbled. "Help!" She was choking, her breath coming in jagged bursts.

The other girls were all squealing, "They're in! They both fell in! Oh, no! Miss Rosy's in the water! Help!"

Sophie struggled to pull her life preserver down so she could get a good, deep breath. Then she lunged forward and gave Miss Rosy's back a big Star Girl push toward the dock. She paddled after her, kicking hard. When Sophie reached the edge of the dock, she tried to heave herself up onto the boards, but her wet life preserver weighed a ton. She floundered in the water, kicking really hard until she managed to scramble onto the dock.

Miss Rosy clung to the edge of the dock, coughing and gasping, trying to catch her breath, her wet hair plastered against her head. She struggled to climb onto the dock but couldn't lift herself out of the water. Sophie reached down to pull her up as two other counsellors hurried down the ramp.

"Hold on there, Rosy!" cried one of them. "Hold on!"

The other counsellor grabbed the back of Miss Rosy's coat while Sophie pulled Miss Rosy's hand. Together they hauled her onto the dock where she collapsed to her hands and knees, fighting for breath.

Finally she stood. "Thanks," she wheezed to Sophie, wiping her nose on the back of her hand. "Thanks a lot."

Sophie wrung the water out of her jacket and nodded. Despite the sunshine, she was shivering hard. Cold water dribbled from her hair and down her neck and back; her sodden pants clung to her legs. She tugged at her wet jacket under the life preserver to draw it closer around her back, then reached into her pocket to squeeze her Star Girl ball. It was gone! She checked her other pocket, then her pants pockets. Nothing! She must have lost it in the water.

Her stomach tightened as she stared over the dockside into the water while the counsellors secured the *Seabird* with ropes. Where was her ball? She didn't see it in the water. It couldn't be lost!

"There, the *Seabird* is all set and secure," one of the counsellors said to Sophie. She was a big, broad woman with round wire-rimmed glasses and very short grey hair. "My, that was a dramatic arrival! So what's your name?"

"Sophie LaGrange," she said, her arms hugging her body as she shook.

"Let's find your suitcase, Sophie, so you can get out of those wet clothes. That was quick thinking, even though you ended up in the water, too. Okay, girls. Out you come now. One at a time please. We don't need anyone else falling into the water. We'll unload you, then get your luggage. Everyone, please hang your life preservers on the rack over there."

Sophie's fingers trembled as she untied her life preserver and hung it on the rack. A cool breeze found her soaked back, and she jumped around and swung her arms, trying to warm up.

She went back to the edge of the dock and peered hopefully into the water again. Still no sign of her Star Girl ball. Would it float? Had it sunk to the bottom? She had never put the ball into water before, so she didn't know what it would do. Did rubber balls sink? The water was so clear she could see right to the rocky bottom covered with swaying green seaweed, white clamshells, and barnacles. Even a few black minnows flitted around. But no bright red Star Girl ball. A puddle of seawater formed around her feet from her cold, dripping jacket and pants. She crossed her arms tightly and shivered some more. Her excitement about this camping trip was fading fast.

Around her the other girls were unloading the boat. Finally she saw her suitcase and her bedroll in its canvas bag. The suitcase was red leather with a big black letter *S* on its side. It was the same one that had travelled all the way from Montreal to the West Coast with her more than a year ago.

"Come on, Sophie, let's get changed out of these wet duds," Miss Rosy urged. "Follow me, kiddo. I'll show you where."

Sophie lifted her suitcase and took one last look into the water. As soon as she changed into some dry clothes, she would zip right back to the dock and search for her Star Girl Super Bounce Ball. She prayed no one else would find it before she did. Or worse, that it would float away!

TWO

Sophie's feet sloshed in her wet shoes as she followed Miss Rosy along the wooden dock and up the ramp, leaving the other campers sorting out their gear. Glumly she stared at her new runners—soaked and probably ruined.

"Thanks for coming after me in the water," Miss Rosy said. "Your name's Sophie, right?"

"Right."

"That was really brave of you, Sophie. Sorry you had to fall in, too." Miss Rosy grinned at her.

Sophie smiled back. "Pretty dumb of me."

Miss Rosy chuckled. "It was dumb of me to fall in the first place!"

They were walking along a path that led past the big log building that Sophie and Elizabeth had noticed earlier. It had several large windows facing the water.

"That's the mess hall," Miss Rosy said.

"Mess hall?"

"We don't actually make a mess there. It's the kitchen and dining area where we eat, and we meet there when it's raining. Otherwise we all meet here at that flagpole."

A tall flagpole with a Union Jack fluttering in the wind was surrounded by a semicircle of low wooden benches and logs. In the centre was a big stone fire pit.

Sophie followed Miss Rosy past the flagpole and along the narrow gravel path, up the hill, to one of the small grey wooden cabins that Elizabeth had hoped weren't where they would be sleeping. This one had a green door and a plaque with the number four above it.

"These cabins are the bunkhouses," Miss Rosy said. "This one's mine, so we can change in here."

They went up two steps and into the cabin. It was quite dim inside after the bright sun of the day, but Sophie could see four double bunks, two along each wooden wall, plus a single bed behind a low screen.

"We get to sleep in bunks!" Sophie started to feel excited again. "I've always wanted to sleep on a top bunk."

"A first time for everything. *Brrr.* Let's get out of these wet duds before we both catch pneumonia." Miss Rosy rummaged through a low chest of drawers. "You can change over there, and I'll change here. This is my room." It wasn't much of a room, just a narrow single bed under a tall window, but the screen made it private and cozy.

Sophie shivered as she looked around the rest of the cabin.

"Hey, it's not all that bad," Miss Rosy said. "After you campers fix it up, it'll look swell. Now you'd better get changed. Pronto."

The wet laces were sticky and tugged as Sophie pulled off her runners and peeled off her wet bobby socks. Dark blue blotches of dye from her new shoes had bled through to the white socks. She lifted her suitcase to one of the bunks along the wall and dug out a pair of shorts, underwear, and a blouse. As she groped for socks, her fingers touched the smooth paper of her secret. Good. They were still there. At the last minute she had sneaked in a small stash of her favourite Star Girl comics.

Maman had told her that comics and toys weren't allowed at camp. But Sophie couldn't bear a whole week without her treasured Star Girl comics, so she had hidden a few under her clothes. She quickly pulled off the rest of her wet clothing and said, "I need to get to the dock."

"What's the matter?" Miss Rosy asked in a muffled voice from behind the screen.

"My Star Girl Super Bounce Ball is missing. I think I must have lost it when I fell into the water."

"Oh, that's too bad, Sophie. You do know you aren't supposed to bring any toys to camp, right?"

"My ball's not a toy. Not really." Sophie quickly pulled on her dry clothes. There, that was better. She felt warmer immediately and stopped trembling.

As Sophie was buckling up her sandals, Miss Rosy asked, "Ready to go?"

"Just about. I'm going back down to the dock to find my ball now."

"You can do that later. Just don't let Miss Bottomly see you, though."

"Miss Bottomly?"

"The camp leader. She was the woman with the grey hair and glasses down at the dock."

Sophie's lips twitched into a grin. *Bottomly.* A perfect name for that broad-bottomed older woman.

"She's pretty nice but really strict about some things, and bringing toys and comics to camp is one of them."

Sophie scattered her extra clothes to hide her Star Girl comics at the bottom of her suitcase. Then she shut the lid firmly.

"Roll up your wet duds and I'll show you where to hang them out to dry," Miss Rosy said. "Don't forget your suitcase and your bedroll."

Sophie bundled her wet clothes into her jacket, put her shoes on top, and followed Miss Rosy out of the cabin.

They were pegging the last of their clothes on a line behind the cabin when another motorboat pulled up to the dock. This one landed without incident, and soon another load of campers and counsellors were climbing up the ramp, laden with suitcases and bedrolls.

"That's the next group," Miss Rosy said. "We'll have forty-two campers altogether this week. Let's go down and meet them."

Picking up her suitcase and bedroll, Sophie followed Miss Rosy toward the dock. This was a great chance to find her ball. She prayed it would be right there bobbing beside the dock where she had fallen in and she could just scoop it right up and hide it in her pocket.

Sophie hurried past the flagpole where the older woman with the broad bottom was standing. She was wearing a grey long-sleeved sweater and a navy camp skirt that stretched across her backside. Several girls were sitting in front of her on the low benches. The woman rang a big school bell, beckoning the girls to come and meet her at the flagpole.

"When you hear that bell," Miss Rosy told Sophie, "you have to drop everything and hightail it to the flagpole or the mess hall as fast as you can. It's the signal for a meeting."

Ah, zut! Sophie thought. Wouldn't she ever have time to go down to the dock to find her ball? Maybe after the meeting was over. She was beginning to feel anxious.

As she looked for a seat, Sophie searched for Elizabeth. She spotted her talking and laughing with a couple of girls, one with long black braids and the other with a bouncing ponytail. It looked as if Elizabeth had already made new friends.

"Quiet, please, everyone," Miss Bottomly said in a big, loud voice, clapping her hands and sternly glancing at all the campers. "Everyone quickly find a seat now and listen up."

There was one empty spot in the semicircle of logs and low benches and that was next to the silent grey girl who had sat beside Sophie on the boat. So she put her suitcase down on the grass and sat on her bedroll.

"First things first," the older woman continued. "A big welcome to you all to Camp Latona and Gambier Island." She and the counsellors clapped. "Now I'd like to introduce you to the staff here at camp and then you'll be assigned to your bunkhouses with your buddies and your counsellor."

There were five counsellors in all. Sophie already knew Miss Rosy, and also Miss Naomi, who had driven the boat from Porteau Cove. The other three counsellors were Miss Bonny, who had red hair and freckles and looked friendly enough, and Miss Linda and Miss Debbie, who both seemed pretty serious. Sophie hoped that she wouldn't have to be in either of their groups.

"And I'm Miss Bottomly," the leader was telling them.

Bottomly. Sophie grinned again and wondered if the woman's first name began with a *B*. If it did, that would be a perfect name for her. Big Bottomly.

"Now, if you have any problems whatsoever during this week, please feel free to come and see me. If you're feeling lonely or homesick, or have a question, my door is always open. Also, I'd like you to meet Mr. Buzz, who is Mr. Jack-of-All-Trades around here, as well as our canoe instructor extraordinaire. And if we ask him very nicely, he might even agree to play his guitar for us sometime."

A robust man with thick glasses and a crew cut waved his guitar at them. He had a bushy moustache that looked like a small animal resting on his upper lip. It twitched when he grinned at them.

"And here's another very important person in our camp," Miss Bottomly added. "Mrs. Carson and her son, Danny."

A slim woman with pink cheeks and hair pulled back into a bun waved and smiled widely at everyone. Holding her hand was a little boy of four or five. He had a mop of blond curls and reminded Sophie of her little brother, Zephram, who was three. The little boy shyly waved at the girls.

"He's cute," a girl near Sophie said.

Sophie nodded but didn't say anything.

"When I call your name, please stand and you'll be given your buddy," Miss Bottomly was saying. "But before I do that, just a word about our buddy system. Each one of you will be responsible for your buddy for the entire week at Camp Latona. If anything happens to her, you must report to me or your counsellor immediately. It is so important that you be with your buddy at all times that if anyone is caught without her buddy at any time, her cabin will automatically lose ten points.

"There are two basic rules at Camp Latona. The first is, always be kind to each other. We don't expect anything else. And the second is, you must stay with your buddy at all times. Gambier is a big island with very few people living here, and we certainly don't want anyone getting lost or hurt. Yes, there are wild animals, including bears, so it's very important that you stay close to camp except when you're hiking with your counsellor. Never, ever, wander off on your own."

Sophie noticed the girls around her staring at one another with big, scared eyes. She tried to catch Elizabeth's attention, but Elizabeth was whispering to the girl with long black braids. Sophie crossed her fingers and hoped that Elizabeth would be her buddy. She *had* to be. Sophie didn't know anyone else.

"Before I call out your names," Miss Bottomly went on, "I'd like you all to remember something else. There's an old saying that I'm sure you've heard before. It's 'A friend in need is a friend indeed.' I hope that this week you'll all make many new friends. Friends you'll keep for a long time. Now the first eight girls whose names I call will be in cabin one with Miss Naomi."

As Miss Bottomly read out eight girls' names from the list, Sophie held her breath. None of the names was hers or Elizabeth's. Sophie felt a little disappointed. She liked Miss Naomi. It would have been fun to be in her cabin for a week.

As Miss Bottomly read out the names of the campers assigned to Miss Rosy's cabin four, Sophie held her breath again. "Please, please," she whispered, crossing her fingers even harder.

Then she heard her name being called. *Yes!* She jumped up. She was to be in cabin four with Miss Rosy. The best! She carried her suitcase and bedroll to where Miss Rosy was waiting. Then Elizabeth's name was called, and Sophie moved eagerly toward her friend.

"And Sophie LaGrange," Miss Bottomly said, "your buddy will be a newcomer to our country. Ginette Berger is from a refugee camp in France. I know you two will get along just fine, since you both speak French."

Sophie's heart fell, and she grimaced. The silent grey girl who had been sitting beside her on the boat was her buddy. Of all the crummy luck! She had to spend all her time for an entire week with someone so disagreeable.

The girl dragged a worn duffle bag and stood beside Miss Rosy.

She didn't even bother to look up at Sophie, or anyone else for that matter.

At least Sophie and Elizabeth were in the same cabin. That was something. Sophie noticed with a pang that Elizabeth's buddy was Margaret Pearson, the girl with long black braids, the girl Elizabeth had been giggling with.

"We're like the two princesses in England," Elizabeth said, arranging the ribbon in her long blond hair and sniffing. "Princess Margaret and Princess Elizabeth."

"Right," Margaret said, her chin in the air. "We're just like royalty."

Sophie glanced at her buddy, Ginette Berger, who shrank back into her raincoat and pulled her hood lower over her pale eyes. *Just great,* Sophie thought.

"Grab your packs and bedrolls, campers," Miss Rosy told them in a loud, jolly voice. "And come along this way." As she led the eight girls up the path to cabin four, she sang, "Pack up your troubles in your old kit bag and smile, smile, smile..."

The girls laughed, and soon they were singing along and marching behind her, swinging their suitcases and bedrolls.

Smile was the last thing Sophie felt like doing. Nothing was turning out as she had planned. She had the grouchiest kid in the whole camp as her buddy for a whole week, and her so-called friend, Elizabeth Proctor, seemed to have a new best friend. And on top of that, she had lost her Star Girl Super Bounce Ball. Sophie looked longingly at the dock, then made a decision. She just had to have her ball. She would sneak back down there the first chance she got. And that was that.

THREE

Miss Rosy stopped in front of the green door of cabin four. "When we get inside," she told the campers, "choose a bunk with your buddy. Then unpack, make your beds, and get the place all comfy and cozy. We have about half an hour before lunch."

The girls crowded into the cabin, prattling with excitement.

"We have to sleep here?" Elizabeth asked, wrinkling her nose and glancing around. "It's so small and dark. Where's our bathroom?"

"You'll find the bathroom in the washroom cabin, which we share with all the girls at camp," Miss Rosy said. "I'll show it to you after you unpack."

"You mean we have to *share* the bathroom?" Margaret said, aghast.

"Yes sirree, bub," Miss Rosy said. "This is camping, remember. Not the fancy-dancy Empress Hotel. So everybody choose a bunk."

Before Sophie could say anything, Ginette Berger threw her

bedroll onto the upper bunk closest to the door.

"Wait, Ginette. Let's choose straws to see who sleeps on the top," Sophie suggested.

Ginette shook her head and scrambled up the ladder, dragging her duffle bag behind her. Sophie would much rather have had a bed near a window, and a chance to sleep on an upper bunk, but Ginette had already decided. It wasn't fair, and Sophie was annoyed that Ginette hadn't even asked her what she wanted.

The other girls were laughing and chattering as they decided where they should go. Margaret and Elizabeth were yapping as if they had known each other for ages and were best friends. Elizabeth was grinning and giggling. She certainly didn't look disappointed about not having Sophie as a buddy.

Sophie kicked the leg of the bunk and dumped her bedroll onto the bed. The drab cabin's army-brown metal bunks and wooden floor soon became strewn with the girls' clothing, blankets, and towels. In contrast, the area behind Miss Rosy's screen was tidy and cheerful, with a low chest of three drawers and a wooden straight-backed chair. A jar of yellow and purple wildflowers sat on the windowsill, a colourful blanket lay on the bed, and bright pictures festooned the wall and screen.

"Fifteen minutes before lunch," Miss Rosy announced. "Hurry and make up your beds, everyone. And for heaven's sake, tidy up. We get points for neatness, you know. Miss Bottomly could spring a cabin inspection on us at any time."

The girls twittered like birds as they stuffed their extra clothes back into their suitcases and smoothed out their blankets, giggling and gabbing away at one another.

Sophie looked at Ginette, who was lying on her bunk and staring blankly at the ceiling. Sighing, Sophie unrolled her blankets onto the grey-and-white-striped mattress. She pushed her suitcase under the bed and remembered what Maman had said about making new friends at camp. Maman had told her the same saying as Miss Bottomly had: "A friend in need is a friend indeed."

Sophie sighed again. Well, that crabby old Ginette Berger was certainly in need. In need of learning some good manners! If only she didn't look so darn grumpy all the time...

The second thing her mother had told her was: "To have a friend, you have to be a friend."

"Okay," Sophie muttered to herself. "I'll try."

A bell rang.

"That's the lunch bell," Miss Rosy said. "Finally! I'm so starving I could eat a horse. What about you guys?"

"I'm starving, too," one girl said, patting her round tummy. It was Margaret, Elizabeth's buddy.

"Me, too!" Elizabeth said. "It's all this fresh air."

"Me, too, me, too!" all the other girls chanted, gathering around Miss Rosy.

"Come on, Ginette," Miss Rosy said to the grey girl on the upper bunk. "Lunchtime."

Sophie waited while Ginette slowly climbed down the ladder from the upper bunk. The girl had taken off her raincoat and was now wearing a woolly pullover sweater. A faded brown camp hat was pulled so low over her forehead that Sophie couldn't see her eyes.

Sophie and Ginette followed the others down the path toward the mess hall. They passed another wooden building with a bright yellow door.

"That's the washroom, if anyone needs it before lunch," Miss Rosy told them.

No one did, so they continued trailing Miss Rosy to the mess hall where they crowded into the big building. It smelled of homemade bread and ginger cookies, which made Sophie's mouth water. The mess hall was a large room with six big wooden tables, each with ten chairs. Along the back wall was a long counter piled with trays of food.

Mr. Buzz, wearing a big white apron, stood behind the counter, and Mrs. Carson was there, as well, adding a few more trays of food. Her little boy stood shyly behind her. Sophie waved at him and smiled. The little boy waved back at her timidly. She felt a pang of homesickness, remembering her little brother, but her stomach growled and her mouth watered even more. She hadn't realized how hungry she was until she saw and smelled all the food.

"Our table's over there in the corner by the windows," Miss Rosy told her girls. "Miss Bottomly will lead us in Grace. Then two of you will get the trays of food from the counter for us."

"Would you like Margaret and me to get the trays?" Elizabeth asked, putting up her hand before anyone else had a chance to volunteer.

"Why, yes. Thank you for offering, Elizabeth," Miss Rosy said, smiling at her.

Elizabeth beamed and patted back her red hair ribbon. She was already up to her teacher's pet tricks.

Sophie moaned and wished she had offered first. She glanced at her buddy Ginette beside her and stroked the tabletop. It was scrubbed wood, smooth and silky to the touch. On the wall behind the counter was a small crucifix and a picture of the Virgin Mary in her blue robes, reminders that the camp was run by Catholic Charities.

"Let's all join hands for Grace," Miss Bottomly said.

Sophie reached out for Ginette's hand, but she kept them folded tightly across her chest. Sophie held Margaret's hand on her other side and joined the girls bowing their heads while Miss Bottomly said Grace. "Bless us, O Lord, and these gifts that we are about to receive from thy bounty. Through Christ, our Lord. Amen."

"Amen," the girls echoed.

Lunch was lemonade and bologna-and-cheese sandwiches on fresh homemade bread, with pickles and raw carrots and celery. For dessert there were crunchy ginger cookies.

"Um, take just two sandwiches at a time, please, Ginette," Miss Rosy said when the girl piled her plate with sandwiches. "We have to leave some for everyone."

Ginette glared at her and put the rest back. After smothering her sandwiches with mustard and ketchup, she stuffed them into her mouth whole. Mustard and ketchup dribbled down her chin, which she wiped off with the back of her hand.

Elizabeth and Margaret exchanged looks and snickered behind their napkins.

Miss Rosy frowned at them. "Some carrots and celery?" she asked Ginette with a polite smile.

Ginette shook her head and reached straight across Sophie's plate for another sandwich. She wolfed it down, as well. She gulped a glass of lemonade and grabbed a stack of cookies from the plate. She ate as if she hadn't had a proper meal for a week.

"Um, two each of the cookies, as well," Miss Rosy told her. "You're so right, Elizabeth. This fresh air has given us all good appetites."

When Miss Rosy looked away to talk to Elizabeth, Ginette sneaked a couple more cookies from the plate and pushed them up her sleeve. Sophie couldn't believe it. What a hog! She nibbled daintily at her sandwich and carrots, feeling she had to be extra polite to make up for her buddy's lack of manners.

Miss Bottomly tapped her cup with a spoon, and the tinkle got everyone's attention. "Thank you, girls," she said when all eyes were on her. "I'd like to tell you our plans for this afternoon. Girls from cabins one and two, you'll be having canoe lessons. Cabins three and four, you're scheduled for swimming lessons. And cabin five, you're on KP."

The girls from cabin five groaned.

"Some people think KP stands for kitchen patrol, but it really means kitchen privileges," Miss Bottomly continued. "I'm sure cabin five will do an excellent job. Mrs. Carson will enjoy their help, and it's a chance for them to earn extra points for their cabin. So girls from cabins one, two, three, and four, meet at the flagpole in forty minutes, at two o'clock, with your towels and your swimming gear. As I said, girls from cabins one and two will have canoe lessons, while cabins three and four will have swimming lessons. At three o'clock we'll switch. Girls from cabins three and four will have their canoe lesson, and cabins one and two will have swimming. Cabin five will join the swimming group when they've finished their KP."

Sophie saw Ginette scowling, but at the mention of canoe lessons for cabins three and four, her face brightened a little. She glanced around at the other girls at the table, then quickly snatched the last few cookies from the tray and shoved them up her sleeve, as well.

Strange, Sophie thought. *For such a skinny little kid she sure has an enormous appetite.*

"You may go back to your cabins now," Miss Bottomly said.

Sophie decided this was a good chance to find her Star Girl ball. She had forty minutes to get back to the dock and make a thorough search. Sophie put her hand in her shorts pocket. It was empty. More than empty. Her pocket was like a deep hole into which all her courage had drained.

As the cabin four girls trooped out of the mess hall behind Miss Rosy, Sophie turned, determined to go down to the dock.

"Come on, girls," Miss Rosy said, looking directly at Sophie. "We'll have plenty of time to go down to the dock later. Right now you should get all your stuff organized, maybe even decorate the cabin a little. Then you have to get your swimming gear ready for your lessons. Oh, and there's something special I want to tell you about."

Sophie couldn't believe it. At this rate her ball would be lost forever. Reluctantly she followed the rest of her cabin mates back to cabin four.

As the girls clattered to get in through the door, Ginette tripped over the ledge and sprawled onto the floor on her hands and knees.

"Ginette!" Miss Rosy cried, rushing to help her. "Are you all right?"

Ginette nodded, blushing. She got to her feet and quickly brushed off her knees.

Margaret and Elizabeth arched their eyebrows at each other as if to say, "What a clumsy dolt!"

Sophie's cheeks burned with embarrassment. She felt a surge of pity.

Thankfully one of the other girls—Sophie thought her name was Betty—changed the subject. "What was the special thing you want to tell us, Miss Rosy?"

"Oh, yes," Miss Rosy said, lowering her voice as if she were telling them a secret.

Sophie leaned forward with the other girls to hear.

"I just found out that there's going to be a contest tonight for the best cabin call, so I thought we could get a head start," Miss Rosy said, her eyes big. "Anybody got any ideas?"

"What's a cabin call?" Elizabeth asked.

"You know, something like, 'Oh, we're all in cabin eight and we're so great!'"

"How about, 'We're in cabin four and we fall on the floor'?" Elizabeth's buddy, Margaret, snickered.

The other girls stared at Ginette and laughed, too. Ginette's cheeks blazed, and she pulled her camp hat lower over her face.

Sophie jumped in front of her buddy and yelled in her loudest voice, "Oh, we're cabin four and our heads are so sore, 'cause we slammed our green door!" Then she couldn't think of anything else to rhyme.

A girl named Peggy called out, "And we're rotten to the core!"

"I love it!" Miss Rosy said. "You guys are so creative. Let's try it all together. From the top now, everyone."

FOUR

Sophie sprinted toward the dock. If she was really quick, she could hunt for her Star Girl ball before their swimming lessons started. Now that the tide was out the sea was low, which made the ramp leading to the dock so steep that she had to hang on to the sides to keep her balance.

"I want everyone in cabins three and four down here at the beach," Miss Bonny said. "Come on, all of you." She gestured toward Sophie.

Grudgingly Sophie left the ramp and trudged behind the rest of the girls down the path to the beach. All the girls were wearing bathing suits and sandals and had towels draped over their shoulders. Everyone except Ginette. She hadn't changed into her bathing suit. She was still wearing the same old brown pants, a dark blue woolly sweater, and the same dumb shiny white shoes tied on with straps.

"Aren't you getting your bathing suit on, Ginette?" Miss Bonny asked.

Ginette shook her head. "No swim," she muttered. It was the first time Sophie had heard her speak. Her voice was low and husky and sounded strange coming from such a small person. Sophie wondered if she was afraid of water or just didn't have a swimsuit.

The girl was crouched on a rock, her camp hat pulled low over her eyes, arms hugging her knees. She looked completely unhappy.

Miss Rosy appeared concerned and gently patted her back. "You can sit and wait here on the rock and watch for now, okay?"

The girl frowned and stared at her feet.

The beach was rocky, but the rocks were smooth for the most part, so they didn't hurt Sophie's bare feet too much as she gingerly followed Miss Rosy and the other girls to the water's edge.

"Now, girls," Miss Bonny cautioned, "when you're swimming, it's especially important to stay with your buddy at all times, no matter what."

Sophie shot a look at Ginette, who was still crouched on a rock.

"It's okay, Sophie," Miss Rosy said. "I'll be your buddy this time."

The swimming lesson wasn't so much a lesson as a free swim, with everyone showing Miss Bonny how far they could swim on their backs, then on their fronts. Sophie splashed around with the other girls in the cool water.

"Don't splash me!" Elizabeth squealed as she tiptoed into the shallow water.

Margaret squealed, too.

"Sorry," Sophie said. "I didn't mean to. You guys should just get wet all over, then you won't feel the splashes so much."

"But the water's so freezing," Elizabeth said.

"It's great once you get used to it," Sophie said, dunking under the water again. "Come on in," she said, spitting out salty water toward Elizabeth.

But Elizabeth shook her head, and she and Margaret ventured in just up to their knees, screeching at each other.

Sophie had learned how to swim the summer before in a small pool at Mackin Park, but that was in freshwater. Swimming in this salty water was easier in a way, because the water seemed to make her float better, but small waves kept rolling her toward the shore. When she licked her lips, they tasted salty. Most of the other girls could swim a bit, and the water wasn't over anyone's head.

"No one is allowed past the end of the ramp," Miss Bonny told them. "The water gets too deep near the dock, and I want to keep my eyes on all of you."

"Let's join hands and sing 'Ring Around the Rosie,'" Miss Rosy said. "Come on, Elizabeth and Margaret."

Sophie held on to Miss Rosy's and Margaret's hands and sang, "Ring around the rosie." At "we all fall down" all the girls dunked under the water. Margaret and Elizabeth grabbed each other and really squealed, but at last they were all wet.

"Okay, show me your stuff," Miss Bonny said. "Show me how far you can swim on your back."

Sophie anxiously waited for an opportunity to slip over to the dock to search for her Star Girl ball. She worried that someone would find it before she did. So when Miss Rosy was watching a group of splashing, laughing girls, Sophie began to make her way toward the dock. She was stopped in her tracks by Miss Rosy calling her back.

"How about showing me how far you can swim on your side, Sophie?"

Disappointed, Sophie waded back to the girls and began swimming. Then, finally, the lesson was over.

"Everyone out of the water now," Miss Bonny called. "Come on, you two," she said to Elizabeth and Margaret, who were flicking water at each other and giggling. "Come and dry off. It's time for your canoe lesson."

"But we just got in!" Margaret protested.

"You'll have plenty of time for swimming this week. So out of the water now," Miss Bonny said firmly.

Sophie bolted out of the water, snatched up her towel, and dried her legs and feet. Then she quickly pulled the towel around her back, shoved her feet into her sandals, and scurried up the beach toward the ramp leading to the dock.

"Hold your horses, Sophie," Miss Rosy called after her. "Wait for the rest of us."

Frustration surged through Sophie. At this rate she would never find her ball! Reluctantly she headed to the flagpole with the other girls.

"Okay, campers," Miss Bonny said, "you must stay with your buddy during this activity, as well. Line up, please."

Sophie stood next to Ginette, who still ignored her. Whenever Sophie glanced at the girl or tried to talk to her, she looked away. Some buddy! Buddies were supposed to be fun. Sophie stared at Elizabeth. Would she and Margaret ever stop giggling together?

In pairs the girls followed Miss Bonny down the ramp, which was still very steep in the low water.

"Hold on to the railings so you won't fall into the drink," Miss Rosy told them.

On the dock Mr. Buzz greeted them with a grin that twitched his small animal moustache. He pushed his glasses up on his nose, clapped his hands, and asked, "Now who's ready for the thrill of a lifetime?"

"Me! Me! Me!" the girls shouted, making the dock sway as they jumped around.

"Okay. But first, a few rules. Number one, never, ever, get into a boat, especially a canoe, without your life preserver. Canoes are tippy, and you never know when one could flip right over and toss you into the water. Without a life preserver to keep you afloat, even the best swimmer would be in danger of drowning."

It was funny to watch him. As he spoke, his furry moustache wobbled and quivered, and his head bobbed up and down so much that it was hard to concentrate on what he was saying.

Sophie forced herself to frown so she wouldn't start giggling, but Elizabeth caught her eye. She grinned and wiggled her eyebrows up and down. The giggles burst out of Sophie's mouth like pop out of a shaken bottle. Elizabeth and Margaret began laughing, too.

"What could possibly be so funny?" Mr. Buzz asked as he and Miss Bonny passed out the bulky orange life preservers.

Sophie rubbed her face and swallowed hard. She gazed into the water and managed to stop laughing. A glint of yellow caught her eye. Was that her Star Girl ball?

"Here's yours, Sophie," Miss Bonny said, passing Sophie a life preserver. "What's so interesting down there in the water?"

"Nothing," Sophie said, pulling the life preserver over her head, crossing the straps in the back, and tying them firmly around her waist in front. "Just a bit of seaweed."

Ginette was tying on her life preserver, as well, though she was still scowling. Was she actually going to participate in this activity? Sophie wondered. That would be a change.

Sophie peered into the water again. When they arrived, their boat had come in about halfway along the dock. That was where her ball must have fallen in. She knelt and leaned over the edge. Bright green seaweed grew on the submerged part of the wooden dock, where two purple starfish and several clumps of black clams were nestled. A small school of shiny minnows flicked their tails and swam into the darkness under the dock. But there was no sign of her ball. It must have sunk to the bottom, or maybe it had drifted under the dock.

"Ah, another bunch of keen canoeists, I see," Mr. Buzz said, rubbing his hands together, wobbling his furry moustache, and bobbing his head. "A bit giggly, but keen. Now be sure you've tied those life preservers nice and tight. Okay, how many do we have here?" The girls all stood in a line as he counted them. "Sixteen. Perfect, since we have eight boats. How many of you have paddled a canoe before?"

Two girls from cabin three who were buddies put up their hands.

"Great!" Mr. Buzz said, bobbing and weaving his head and twitching his moustache.

Sophie tried not to gawk at him. She knew she would start giggling again if she did, so she stared hard at the canoes instead. Lined up in a row along the dock, they were varnished wood inside and painted green on the outside, with two wooden seats in each boat, one in front and the other toward the back.

"You two can be our volunteers for the demonstration," Mr. Buzz said to the girls from cabin three.

The girls stepped forward to get into a boat.

"When you get in or out of a boat, always do it one person at a time, and always step right in the middle of the boat. Perfect. You're doing great." Mr. Buzz handed a wooden paddle to each girl. "The proper way to hold a canoe paddle is one hand here, about a foot down from the top, and your other hand right here on the top. That way you won't end up socking yourself in the nose like this. *Oof!*" As he demonstrated, his moustache almost fell off his upper lip. All the girls, including Sophie, exploded with laughter.

"What a pile of gigglers you girls are!" he said. "All right. With your buddies I want you to get into your boats, one girl in front at the bow, and one in the back at the stern. Don't forget to step into the middle of the canoe. One at a time. Excellent, excellent. A bunch of pros."

Sophie wasn't sure if Ginette was going to join in, so she watched her. Ginette had tied on the life preserver and she had practised holding the paddle correctly. Then, without any hesitation, she climbed into the front of a canoe.

Stepping gingerly into the canoe, too, Sophie moved to the back seat as the canoe rocked precariously in the water. She sat down quickly and gripped her paddle. Balancing in the canoe was sort of like balancing when riding a bike.

"Now, you've probably noticed that these boats are much smaller than your regular canoe," Mr. Buzz was saying as each pair settled into a boat. "They're singles and usually paddled by one person, but we find they're perfect for kids like you to learn. Two more bits of advice. You can sit down on the seat and paddle if the water's calm, but you'll find that the boat will feel more stable if you kneel. And the other thing is—don't go past the end of the dock or out of this cove. Just paddle around here in the shallow water until you get a feel for the boat. Hey! You're all doing just great! Oh, one other thing. You should always paddle on opposite sides. If the front person paddles on the right side, that's the starboard, the back person should be paddling on the left. We call that the port. That way your boat won't be so tippy."

Sophie switched to her left side, since Ginette was paddling hard on the right.

"This is so fun!" Elizabeth squealed.

"Major fun!" Margaret squealed back, almost bashing into Sophie and Ginette's canoe.

Sophie had to paddle furiously backward to avoid a crash. The most difficult part so far was avoiding smashing into the other canoes in the narrow cove.

After they paddled around for a while, Mr. Buzz said, "Okay, you guys. Time's up. Paddle over here to the dock and we'll help you out. One person at a time."

Ginette kept on paddling like a windmill in a storm. Each time Sophie tried to aim the boat toward the dock, Ginette hurriedly paddled in the other direction.

"We've got to go back to the dock!" Sophie shouted at her. "Look, all the other girls are getting out now."

Ginette didn't turn around or even acknowledge Sophie.

Mr. Buzz called out to them, "Hey, you two. Come on in. Now."

"Come on, Ginette," Sophie said. "Stop paddling us away from the dock." She tried to make the canoe turn, but it wouldn't go where she wanted it to.

Mr. Buzz had to call them again. Finally Ginette started to paddle toward the dock. They were the last boat in. Sophie couldn't understand why Ginette was acting like that.

Miss Bonny held their boat steady against the side of the dock while Sophie got out, followed by Ginette. "You certainly liked that canoeing, I see," Miss Bonny said, raising her eyebrows at Ginette.

Ginette scowled as she handed her the life preserver.

"It was really fun," Sophie said. "Can we go paddling again tomorrow?"

"Tomorrow and every day this week," Miss Bonny said. "You'll all be experts by the end of the week."

Ginette was looking so intently at the canoes that she seemed unaware of anyone around her.

"What are you thinking about?" Sophie asked, hoping the girl would begin talking to her.

Ginette shook her head and shrugged. "Nothing," she muttered in her strange, low voice.

FIVE

"Come on, campers," Miss Rosy said. "You'll have to hustle out of your wet duds and into the shower before supper. And, yes, everyone does have to have a shower. Hustle, hustle, hustle! Twenty-four skidoo!"

Sophie trooped back to cabin four with her cabin mates for a dry towel and a change of clothes. Instead of heading straight for the shower, though, she had to wait for Ginette to rifle through her battered duffle bag for dry clothes.

"You have to shower before supper, Ginette," Sophie told her when it seemed as if the girl was just going to sit around on her bunk. "Miss Rosy said everyone has to have a shower. Come on. I don't want to wait all day." Sophie hopped from one foot to the other impatiently.

Big grey clouds had rolled in to cover the sky, and the wind had picked up. Although it wasn't late, the day had grown so dark that they had flicked on the light in the cabin. It was a single bulb suspended from the ceiling, and it cast swaying shadows on the wooden floor.

Finally Ginette reluctantly climbed down from her bunk and headed for the door. She looked grumpier than ever as she stomped along the path to the washroom cabin where the showers and toilets were. Her camp hat was pulled low over her forehead.

The washroom was warm and steamy when they entered by the freshly painted yellow door. The sharp smell of disinfectant tickled Sophie's nose. She rubbed her nose with the back of her hand. The floor was grey concrete, and there was a long row of toilet stalls across from a row of sinks and one big shower area with six taps and six shower heads. About ten girls were yelping and giggling as they showered together in the steam under the hot water.

Another bunch of girls from cabin five were jostling one another, combing out their wet hair in front of the fogged-up mirror above the sinks. One of them turned and stared at Ginette, then she snickered and said in a loud whisper, "DP. Look. There's the DP."

One of the girls covered her mouth and appeared shocked that she would call anyone such a derogatory name, but the other girls just giggled.

Ginette's cheeks burned.

How dare they! Sophie thought. DP was the worst thing you could call anyone. It stood for displaced person, and only the most down-and-out people who had no home or nowhere to go in the whole world were called displaced persons.

She clamped her hands on her hips and glared at the rude girls with her mad Star Girl stare. Most of the girls just turned away and continued primping their hair in the mirror. Only a couple of them looked embarrassed.

Sophie knew Ginette had heard them. The back of the girl's neck had turned red, and her shoulders were sunken.

"Looks like this is where we hang up our towels and clothes so they won't get wet from the shower," Sophie said to Ginette in a loud voice, as though nothing had happened.

Ginette shook her head.

Sophie lowered her voice and said, "But you have to have a shower, Ginette. Everyone has to. Miss Rosy said."

Ginette shook her head and looked away.

"Well, I'm going to have one. You can just wait here then," Sophie said, pulling off her bathing suit and dropping it onto the floor beneath a peg holding her towel and dry clothes. Elizabeth was already in the shower, so Sophie stood next to her.

The gush of warm water on her head felt lovely. She let it stream down her hair, the back of her neck, and over her shoulders. She didn't have a shower at home, so this was a real treat. Elizabeth was rubbing shampoo into her hair.

"Can I borrow some of your shampoo, Liz?" Sophie asked.

"Sure. Here."

It didn't take much shampoo to get a good lather in Sophie's short, curly hair. As she was rinsing out the shampoo, Ginette crept timidly into the shower beside her. Sophie was puzzled. Ginette had kept on her underwear and a long-sleeved grey undershirt.

A girl on the other side of Sophie snorted at Ginette.

"Hey, Liz," Sophie said loudly to Elizabeth so Ginette wouldn't hear the tittering, "can Ginette borrow a bit of your shampoo, too?"

"Sure. Don't use it all, though. It has to last me the whole week."

"Do you want some shampoo?" Sophie held the bottle out to Ginette. She nodded. Sophie tried to pour a little onto her hair, but a big blob came out. Ginette rubbed it in, and soon her head was covered with mounds of suds.

"Just rinse under the tap," Sophie told her.

Ginette stood under the tap for ages, but there were still suds in her hair. Finally she left the shower area, took her towel and clothes into one of the toilet cubicles, and locked the door with a loud click.

"She sure is modest," Elizabeth said, towelling her hair.

"She's just not used to all this camp stuff yet, I guess," Sophie said, pulling her pants and sweater on over her underwear.

"Well, she'll never fit in if she doesn't get used to it," Margaret sniffed, patting her braids dry with a towel.

As they were hanging their wet bathing suits and towels on the clothesline behind their cabin, the supper bell rang, so they all tramped over to the mess hall. And still Sophie hadn't had a chance to go down to the dock to hunt for her Star Girl ball.

"Spaghetti! Yum! Spaghetti and meatballs," Sophie said, slurping up a long, wet tomatoey noodle. "This is the best spaghetti I've ever tasted in my whole entire life!"

Sophie and the other girls at the table dug into their suppers with gusto, but Ginette beat them all. Her pale, straight hair was still wet from the shower and stuck out from the sides of her head. At least she wasn't wearing the same old camp hat.

For dessert there were ginger cookies again, with squares of wobbly orange jelly in little glass bowls. When Ginette got her jelly, she poked at it with her spoon and looked puzzled when it jiggled. It was as if she had never seen jelly before. After tasting it tentatively with the tip of her tongue, she sucked it up noisily, smacked her lips, and looked around for more. Her eyes were shiny with eagerness, and her damp hair stuck out like pale whiskers. The other girls fell quiet and stared. Margaret giggled behind her cupped hand and whispered to Elizabeth, who started to giggle back but stopped when she saw Sophie glaring at her.

Sophie knew the girls were thinking: *Just look at that dumb* DP.

Looks as if she's never seen jelly before. She doesn't even know how to eat it.

"Want another cookie, Ginette?" she asked purposefully as she passed her the plate of cookies.

Ginette took two. She quickly shoved one into her mouth, and the other disappeared up her sleeve. Sophie couldn't figure out the girl's strange behaviour.

After supper Sophie was about to sprint away to the dock to look for her ball when Miss Bottomly announced that it was cabin four's turn for KP. *Of all the rotten luck!* Sophie thought.

While the rest of the campers filed out of the mess hall and had free time, the girls from cabin four had to stay and wash the dishes, cutlery, pots, and pans. Then they had to dry them and put them away, ready for the next meal.

"Why do we have to do all the cleanup?" a girl named Brenda complained, flicking back her ponytail.

"They should hire maids to do this work," Margaret said.

"Each cabin will have a turn doing KP," Miss Rosy told them. "Don't worry. And if we do a good job, we could earn ten extra points. So, campers, let's do our very best."

"What is all this points stuff about, anyway?" Margaret asked.

"The cabin with the most points at the end of the week will be the grand champions, and everyone in the cabin will get a prize."

"What prize?" Elizabeth asked.

"Wait and see," Miss Rosy said. "It'll be something really, really good."

"That we get to keep?"

"Of course. Now, who wants to wash and who wants to dry?"

Before Sophie could volunteer, all the jobs had been taken. Of course, Ginette hadn't volunteered for anything. Sophie hoped that she could slip away unnoticed to the dock.

"Here, Sophie," Miss Rosy said, handing her a damp cloth and a broom. "You and Ginette can tidy the dining area. Wipe the tables and sweep under them so everything is clean and neat."

Sophie gave Ginette the cloth and showed her how to wipe off the tables. "*Comme ça. Nettoyez toutes les tables,*" she said in French, telling the girl to clean all the dining tables.

Ginette blinked her pale eyes, seemingly puzzled. She wiped one of the tables. "*Comme ça?*" she asked with just a ghost of a smile playing on her lips.

"*Oui. Juste comme ça,*" Sophie replied, smiling back at her as she began to sweep the floor. Mrs. Carson's little boy, Danny, was there. Sophie smiled at him, too.

"Want to play hide-and-seek with me?" he asked Sophie.

"We can't now," Sophie said. "It's cleanup time. Would you like to hold the dustpan for me?"

"Sure," he said. "I know the best hiding places on the island."

"Maybe we could play sometime tomorrow," she said. "Let's get this dust under the counter now. You're a very good helper, you know that, Danny?"

He grinned and followed her around, carrying the dustpan and holding it whenever she asked him.

By the time they were finished cleaning the dining room, the wind had picked up and was blowing hard outside. The steady drumming of rain pounded the metal roof.

Miss Rosy stared out the window. "Just look at that rain. No campfire for us tonight."

"Ah, but a campfire would be the best. What will we do instead?" Margaret asked, pushing one of her braids back over her shoulder.

"We'll have our evening meeting in here. It'll be lots of fun. It's almost time for inspection, and all the girls from the other cabins will soon be here. Sophie, could you and Ginette move the tables to the sides of the room? We need enough space for everyone to gather around the centre."

Sophie and Ginette, with Danny's help, had just finished moving the tables when Miss Bottomly came in. "And how are we doing, girls?" she puffed, out of breath.

"We're all done," Miss Rosy said proudly.

Miss Bottomly polished her glasses and checked under the tables to see if the floor had been swept properly. She leaned over so much that her knickers showed. Sophie looked away quickly. She wished she had someone she could giggle with, but Ginette was busy positioning a row of chairs and, of course, Elizabeth was off with Margaret.

Miss Bottomly confirmed that all the cups and glasses and plates shone from their places on the shelves. "Everything looks spick-and-span to me. Ten points for you, cabin four," she announced, writing in her notebook.

"Hooray!" the girls of cabin four cried.

"And just in time, too," Miss Bottomly said. "Here come the rest of the girls."

Sophie gazed out the window at the bleak sky. She would never get down to the dock to search for her ball! Maybe she could after the meeting? Although by then it would probably be too dark to see anything.

SIX

The girls moved the rest of the chairs into a semicircle, facing the windows. Then they all took their seats, chattering away in anticipation.

Sophie had to sit in the back row beside Ginette, who remained as silent as ever. Sophie felt left out of all the socializing. She looked longingly at Elizabeth who was, as usual, the centre of a lively discussion.

"Can I sit beside you?" Danny asked Sophie.

"Sure thing, buddy," she said, patting the seat next to her.

Miss Bottomly stood in front of the girls, smoothing down her skirt. She held up her hands for silence. "Thank you, girls!" she boomed. "Well, here we are. Our first evening together at camp. Too bad it's raining, but we'll have a good time nonetheless. First, we're going to have a contest for the best cabin cheer. So get together with the other members of your cabin and start thinking. Your cheer should be peppy and cheerful. Mrs. Carson, Mr. Buzz, and I will be the judges. I'll give you—" she paused and consulted her watch "—twenty minutes to get it ready."

"Can our counsellors help us?" a tall girl from cabin five asked.

"No. You're on your own. The counsellors will be busy getting a surprise ready for you. In fact, you counsellors may leave now."

As Miss Rosy left, she said, "Good luck to you, girls," and gave them a thumbs-up sign.

"Now, when I blow my whistle like this," Miss Bottomly said, "that means your time is up. Starting now."

All the campers from cabin four huddled around Elizabeth and Margaret. Danny huddled with them.

"Anyone have any ideas?" Elizabeth said. She had her camp notebook and pencil poised in the air. She was as organized and bossy as ever.

"I liked the one we started this afternoon," Margaret said. "Maybe we should try to think of some more words to rhyme with four."

"Door, floor, bore, sore, more, store, core!" the girls shouted.

"Okay, okay," Elizabeth said, jotting the list of words in her camp notebook as fast as the girls called them out.

"How about starting, 'Oh, we're not a bore, 'cause we're cabin four'?" Brenda suggested.

Elizabeth nodded. "I like it."

"We need a couple more lines," someone else said.

Ginette just sat there, her eyes flitting from one girl's face to another, then staring out the windows at the wet night.

Sophie felt she had to try extra hard to make up for her buddy not contributing, but she was stuck. She couldn't think of a third line.

"How about, 'We yell for some more, 'cause we're rotten to the core'?" Margaret finished.

Miss Bottomly said, "Five more minutes, girls."

The girls all squealed.

"What have we got so far?" Brenda asked.

Elizabeth cleared her throat and read, "We've got a green door, so we're not a bore, and we yell for some more, 'cause we're rotten to the core. We're all in cabin four."

"We could say it all together, then end up with our hands in the air and yell, 'Yeah!'" Brenda said.

Miss Bottomly blew her whistle. "Time's up, girls. Let's hear your cheers. We'll start with cabin one. Come on up, girls."

The eight girls from cabin one marched up to the front of the semicircle of chairs. The tallest girl was standing at the end. She nodded and they began. "Oh, we're cabin one, and we're the one on the run, 'cause we all like to have fun."

Everyone clapped politely. Sophie didn't think they were very good. Certainly not loud enough. Certainly not as good as cabin four.

"Thank you, girls," Miss Bottomly said. "Let's hear from the girls in cabin two now."

The girls from cabin two gathered. The rest of the girls watched a short red-headed girl who held a paper. "Here's ours," she said.

"Two, two, you want to know who? That's us, that's who. Yeah, cabin two!"

Again everyone clapped politely.

Way too short, Sophie thought.

Then it was cabin three's turn. "Oh, who can that be? Is it a tree? Is it the sea? No, it's me, and I'm in cabin three."

"Well done, girls!" Miss Bottomly said. "It's amazing what you can come up with in just twenty minutes. Now, let's hear what the girls from cabin four have for us."

Sophie swallowed hard and followed Margaret and Elizabeth to the front.

"Can I come, too?" Danny asked.

"Sure thing," Sophie said. "You can stand right beside me. Come on, Ginette."

But Ginette just sat there, frowning.

"Come on, it's our turn," Sophie hissed at her.

Ginette frowned and shook her head.

"You *have* to. Come on," Sophie said, tugging at her sleeve.

But Ginette shook her head again and didn't budge.

Finally Sophie left her and joined the other girls and Danny. They had all gathered around Elizabeth, who was consulting her notebook.

"Okay, ready?" Elizabeth said. "Let's go. One, two, three, four…"

"We've got a green door," the girls from cabin four cried, "so we're not a bore. And we ask for some more, 'cause we're rotten to the core. We're all in cabin four. Yeah!"

Sophie shouted out in a loud voice, especially the "Yeah!" part. Danny yelled, too. Sophie again felt she had to make up for the fact that Ginette hadn't joined them.

The audience clapped. They seemed to like it a lot.

"Thank you, cabin four," Miss Bottomly said. "Just a reminder. We're expecting everyone from each cabin to participate. One more to go. Girls from cabin five, your turn."

Sophie thought that if it wasn't for Ginette they would have had a good chance of winning.

Cabin five was a bigger cabin and had ten girls instead of eight. And they were an older bunch, mostly eleven- and twelve-year-olds instead of ten- and eleven-year-olds. The girls all stood in a straight line across the front. Sophie couldn't see anyone who seemed to be in charge. No one was holding a paper. They started together by marching on the spot. "If you want to dive and feel really alive and not live in a hive, you gotta come to cabin five. F-I-V-E! Five! Five! Five!"

They all shouted in strong, clear voices and ended their cheer by stamping loudly and throwing their hands into the air.

Oh-oh, Sophie thought. *They're good, all right.*

The three judges consulted for a few moments while the campers waited expectantly, whispering to one another excitedly.

Miss Bottomly stood and smoothed down her wrinkled skirt. "We're very impressed by the obvious talent here. Everyone did a great job, and on such short notice, too. You've made our job very difficult, but there was one cabin that had the enthusiastic participation from every single member. So we've decided that the winner of the cabin cheer and ten extra points for their cabin is...cabin five."

"Hooray!" the girls from cabin five cheered.

"They think they're so smart," Elizabeth said, her teeth clenched. "We'll get them next time. Just wait."

"That's right," Margaret said. "Just wait."

Sophie felt the eyes of her cabin mates glaring at her and Ginette. They were blaming Ginette because she hadn't participated. Sophie didn't know where to look. She felt angry and embarrassed.

A loud knock startled her, and she jumped. Danny squealed and hid behind Sophie's chair. Ginette screamed, too, and ducked behind Margaret, who was sitting in front of her.

"Oh, my! Whoever could that be?" Miss Bottomly said.

Mr. Buzz pulled the door open. Ginette cowered in fear, whispering, *"Non, non."*

Two bedraggled figures tumbled through the door. They were dressed in ripped pants and coats, and their faces were covered with soot. Sophie's heart stopped thudding as she recognized the two. It was Miss Rosy and Miss Bonny. Miss Rosy was wearing an old overcoat with the collar pulled up, and Miss Bonny sported a blond wig and had a big umbrella that dripped rain onto the floor.

Danny left Sophie's chair and scooted over to sit on his mother's lap.

Sophie tried to calm Ginette, "It's just Miss Rosy and Miss Bonny. They're pretending."

But Ginette gaped with huge eyes at the two counsellors. She cringed in her chair behind Margaret. Sophie was about to try to reassure her, but the two counsellors began running around in a panic and screaming.

"Oh, help us!" Miss Rosy shouted. "You've got to save us!" She flailed her arms.

"Save you? Save you from what?" Miss Bottomly asked, a look of grave concern on her face.

Ginette appeared to grow smaller as she slumped even lower.

"They're all after us!" Miss Bonny exclaimed. "They'll catch us! They want our map! They're going to steal it!"

"What map?" Miss Bottomly asked.

"The map to the treasure," both counsellors replied.

"What treasure?"

"The treasure that—"

Another loud bang shook the door, and the counsellors jumped.

Ginette slipped to the floor and curled into a tight, frightened ball with her arms over her head. Sophie knelt beside her and patted her back gently. Ginette's back was shaking.

"C'est rien, Ginette. C'est juste une histoire," Sophie murmured into the girl's ear over and over. She couldn't see the action now because they were hidden behind the chairs. But she heard Mr. Buzz open the door again.

"Now what?" he asked.

Sophie peeked over Margaret's shoulder. Two more rough-looking characters, both wearing big black gum boots and raincoats, barged through the door. One of them wore an old brown felt hat with a dripping brim and yelled, "Hey, you two. Give us back our map!"

"Your map?" Miss Bonny said. "It's not your map. We found it fair and square! So there!"

"Yes, finders keepers, losers weepers. Losers, losers!" Miss Rosy chanted, jumping up and down. She took a crumpled paper from an inner pocket in her overcoat and waved it in front of the character wearing the dripping felt hat.

Felt Hat grabbed the paper but slipped on the wet floor, ripping the map in two.

"Look what you've done!" Miss Rosy cried. "Our treasure map is all ripped up. Now none of us will ever find the treasure."

The two other characters fell to the floor, sobbing "Boo-hoo, boo-hoo!" in really loud voices.

"Regardes, Ginette. C'est Mademoiselle Rosy." Sophie told Ginette, pulling her up.

Ginette lifted her head and nervously watched the events, clutching Sophie's sweater tightly.

One of the counsellors sprang up. Sophie thought it was Miss Naomi. She said, "Listen, you guys, maybe we can glue the map together, then we can all share the treasure."

"Hey, that's a good idea!" Miss Rosy said. "But let's hurry and get to Treasure Island before all those other guys do."

"What guys?" the other counsellors cried.

"Those guys," Miss Rosy said, pointing at the audience.

"You're right!" Miss Naomi said. "Into the boats and man your stations, sailors!"

As the four raced out of the mess hall, one of them yelled, "And the last one out's a rotten egg!"

The campers all shouted and clapped. Sophie tried to pull Ginette back up to sit in her chair. "It's okay, Ginette," she whispered.

"You see. It wasn't real. *C'est une histoire comique.* They were just playing a joke. A funny joke."

But Ginette shook her head and wouldn't get up off the floor.

"That was great! Come on back and give us a bow," Miss Bottomly called after the departing counsellors.

"See, Ginette, they're coming back in. It was just Miss Rosy and the other counsellors," Sophie said, urging Ginette to get up.

The four counsellors trooped back into the mess hall and joined Miss Bottomly. They pulled off their funny hats, wigs, and floppy moustaches and bowed low. Miss Naomi, Miss Bonny, Miss Linda and, last of all, Miss Rosy.

The campers hooted and clapped some more. Ginette seemed to relax as the characters became the counsellors again. Slowly she slipped back onto her chair. Sophie hoped no one had noticed that Ginette had been such a scaredy-cat.

Miss Bottomly started singing, "For they're jolly good fellows, for they're jolly good fellows." All the campers joined in. Sophie sang the loudest, but Ginette wouldn't open her mouth.

"Well, that's it for tonight, girls," Miss Bottomly said when the song was finished. "We've all had a long day. So it's beddy-byes for everyone. Lights out at nine o'clock. That's when our generator goes off, so be sure to be in bed with your flashlights before then. The only light that stays on is an oil lamp in the washroom cabin. A storm has been forecast tonight—very windy and wet—so be sure that all the cabin windows and doors are tightly closed. Now let's see which cabin will be dismissed first."

The girls marched out after their counsellors and along the path back to their cabins. Sophie's hands felt restless in her empty pockets. She gazed longingly at the dock. Despite the rain, it might still be light enough to see into the water if she went right away. But it would be pitch-dark soon. Maybe she could sneak away with her flashlight. When they got back into the cabin, she got her flashlight out of her suitcase and followed Ginette and the other girls to the washroom cabin with their toothbrushes and extra towels. Their other towels that were on the clothesline had been soaked by the rain, and someone had pinned them all up on drying racks lining a wall in the washroom cabin.

Suddenly someone screeched from inside the washroom. "Look! It jumped under the sink!"

Girls cowered around the door. Ginette ducked behind a bush.

"What is it?" Sophie asked as she poked her head into the washroom.

"Something jumped right out at me," Elizabeth squealed, flapping her elbows. "Something huge! Then it went under that sink."

Sophie peeked into the darkness under the sink.

"Croak!"

"Ha! It's just a little frog," Sophie said. She soon caught the frog in her cupped hand. Some of the girls yelped again and backed away.

"Nothing to be afraid of," Sophie told them. "It's just a little Pacific tree frog. I bet plenty of them live around here. You can tell he's a Pacific tree frog because of this dark stripe from his nostril to his eye, then down to his armpit. Can you see that?" She opened her hand, and shiny black eyes peered out at the girls. They leaned closer.

"And look," Sophie said. "He's got tiny suction cups at the end of his fingers. Oh, he's so cute! Look, Ginette." Sophie felt good. All the girls were crowding around her for a change.

But Ginette wouldn't budge.

"You're right," Margaret said. "He is cute, but I wouldn't want to hold him. Doesn't he feel all slimy?"

"Not at all," Sophie said. "He just tickles a little." The frog opened his flap of a mouth and gave a high-pitched croak again. "He's just lost in here and wants to go back to his tree outside." Sophie gently carried him out and set him down carefully on a nearby bush.

"How come you're such an expert about frogs?" Margaret asked when Sophie came back into the washroom. "You're like some kind of frog girl."

"We studied frogs in science at school last year," Sophie told her. "And once I even had a couple frogs for pets."

"We didn't do anything that interesting in science at our school," Margaret said.

Sophie washed her hands and face, then squirted toothpaste on her toothbrush and brushed her teeth. Out of the corner of her eye she saw that Ginette was brushing her teeth, as well. When Sophie finished, she followed the other girls back to cabin four.

Everyone looked at the thick wet brush beside the path, hoping to spot a small green Pacific tree frog. They didn't see one, but they could hear high-pitched croaks. Sophie forgot about going down to the dock to search for her ball until she reached the cabin. Was there time to go now before bedtime?

She tucked her flashlight under her arm and was about to leave when Miss Rosy announced, "Five minutes until lights out. Everyone in bed. Get all comfy and cozy."

Ah, zut! Double zut! Sophie thought. She sighed and rolled her damp towel around her flashlight for a pillow.

Sophie pulled on her nightgown and quickly crawled under the covers before anyone noticed that her nightgown was decorated with dancing Christmas reindeers. She hadn't wanted to bring along her warm winter flannelette nightgown, but Maman had insisted, saying that the nights on the island might be too cold for her thin summer baby-doll pajamas. She wished she had thought of packing a proper pillow. Her rolled-up towel was damp and lumpy over the flashlight. She tossed and turned, trying to find a comfortable position.

Girls were whispering and giggling in their bunks, and Ginette moved restlessly in the bunk above. Sophie took a deep breath, and suddenly tiredness swept over her like a fog. She could barely keep her eyes open.

"Good night, troop!" Miss Rosy called out from behind her screen. "Sleep tight. Don't let the bedbugs bite."

Sophie inhaled deeply again, but she couldn't even get her lips open to say good-night back. It seemed like forever since she had left home that morning. It sounded as if everyone else in the cabin was exhausted, as well. There were just a few muffled, sleepy "Good night" replies.

SEVEN

The next morning the weather was cool and overcast, but it had stopped raining. The ferns and bushes along the path to their cabin were shiny and green after the night rain.

"Do we all have to go on the hike?" Margaret whined.

"Yes, we do," Miss Rosy said. "It's not really warm enough this morning to go swimming in the cove, but it's perfect weather for a good hike up to the lake."

"Couldn't we go paddling in the canoes instead?" Elizabeth asked.

"The girls from cabins one and two are doing that. We'll have our turn later if we get back from our hike on time. Come on, let's hurry and get our teeth brushed and our cabin all spick-and-span. Then we can come back to the mess hall and get our picnic supplies. First cabin back always gets the best supplies, so let's step on it, troop."

The girls rushed through brushing their teeth except for Ginette. Sophie had to wait for her as usual.

"Come on, Ginette," she nagged. "Miss Rosy said we've got to hurry. Everyone else is finished."

Sophie was hoping to slip down to the dock to look for her Star Girl Super Bounce Ball. Although after the stormy night, it probably had drifted out to sea. Maybe it had floated all the way to Japan by now. Sophie couldn't stand thinking about that. She just *had* to get her ball back.

When they returned to the cabin, Miss Rosy was again urging the girls to hurry. "Brenda and Betty, your clothes are all over the place. What a mess! Clean it up. Everyone, hurry and change into your bathing suits and grab your towels. We want to get good picnic supplies. First come, first served, you know."

"But why do we need our bathing suits to go on a hike?" Margaret asked.

"The lake has the best swimming on the island. Even on a cloudy day like this the water there will be as warm as the water in a bathtub."

Sophie took off her sweater, shorts, and underwear, and skinned on her bathing suit. It was still damp from swimming and getting rained on the previous day and made her shiver. She pulled her sweater and shorts over top and straightened her bedroll. When she piled her extra clothes into her suitcase, she felt the bottom. Yes! Her Star Girl comics were still there. She hadn't had a second to read them since coming to the island. Sophie patted them and thought again about her Star Girl ball. She just had to get to the dock to search for it. Sophie started out the door, determined to find it right now.

"Just a minute, Sophie," Miss Rosy said. "Take your jacket. It might rain before we get back. And wait for the rest of us."

Sophie went back for her jacket.

"Okay, everyone ready?" Miss Rosy asked. "Let's go." She led the cabin four girls along the trail to the mess hall. Sophie gazed longingly at the water. She imagined her ball right there, bouncing against the edge of the dock, waiting for her to pick it up.

In the mess hall, picnic supplies were laid out on the counter. For each cabin there were two piles of fresh buns wrapped in wax paper, a bowl of hard-boiled eggs, nine oranges, five canteens of water, and a large, delicious-looking banana loaf.

"How do we carry all this stuff?" Betty asked.

"Here are some drawstring bags," Miss Rosy said. "Let's divide it all up. So who wants to carry what?"

Before anyone could answer, Ginette took the banana loaf and slipped it into a drawstring bag.

"I'll take one of those water canteens, I guess," Margaret said. "At least it's got a carry strap."

"I'll take one, too," Elizabeth said. "Imagine having to carry your own drinking water all the way up a mountain."

Miss Rosy raised her eyebrows.

"I'll take the oranges," Sophie said.

"Thank you, Sophie," Miss Rosy said. "Buns, anyone else?"

The other girls each took the buns and eggs, and the extra water canteens.

"I think we're all set to go," Miss Rosy said. "Don't forget your drinking cups."

Each girl took a tin cup from the pile and put it into her own pocket.

While they were getting loaded up, Sophie saw little Danny Carson in a red sweater, peeking out at them from behind the door leading to the kitchen. She smiled and waved at him, and he waved and grinned back.

"Can you play hide-and-seek now?" he asked her.

"We're going on a hike now, but maybe we could play later when we get back," Sophie told him.

Danny followed the girls as they walked to the flagpole where Miss Bottomly gave the girls from cabins three, four, and five last-minute instructions for their hikes. "You must stay with your group and especially with your buddies. I don't want to frighten you, but there have been recent sightings of bears around the island. Generally the island bears are very shy and won't approach a group of people, but we still have to be careful. It's very important for you to stay with your group at all times, and make plenty of noise. Now that shouldn't be too difficult for you."

Elizabeth and Margaret glanced at each other with big eyes.

"You'll all have a great time, I'm sure," Miss Bottomly continued. "And we'll see you back here this afternoon."

"Okay, troop, let's go," Miss Rosy said. She led the girls along the path past the cabins and onto the lake trail, following the girls from the other cabins. Margaret and Elizabeth hiked right behind her.

Sophie wanted to walk with Elizabeth and Margaret, but Ginette hung back. She halted to buckle the straps on her shiny white shoes, so Sophie had to stop and wait for her while all the other girls went on ahead.

"Come on, Ginette. We're supposed to stick with our group. I don't want to be left behind."

Finally Ginette was ready. Sophie slung the bag of oranges over one shoulder and her towel over the other, and they headed up the trail, which went through high bushes and ferns still wet from the night rain. The rest of the girls were so far ahead now that Sophie couldn't see them.

As they turned the corner to go into the woods, Sophie glimpsed something red out of the corner of her eye. "Was that Danny Carson with his red sweater?" she asked Ginette.

Ginette shrugged.

"I hope he's not following us," Sophie said. "He could get lost out here." She turned back and looked hard, but she didn't spot anyone. "Danny!" she called into the bushes. "Don't you dare try to follow us. Go on straight back down the hill and see your mother. What should we do?" she asked Ginette.

Ginette merely shrugged again and turned away.

Sophie knew they shouldn't stop. If they did, they would be left behind. She took one last look down the trail and into the bushes, but now she didn't see anything red. Maybe she had imagined it. She turned and hurried along the trail to catch up with the other girls. She was almost running, the heavy bag of oranges bouncing against her legs. Ginette jogged behind her.

"Finally," Sophie mumbled to herself, "she's listening to me."

As they hiked up the narrow trail, Sophie peered nervously past the thick ferns and into the bushes, looking for the bears Miss Bottomly had mentioned. There was no sign of them, thank goodness. She reached into her jacket pocket where her Star Girl ball should have been. Her heart thudded. She was always braver when she could feel the ball.

"Come on, Ginette, we've got to hurry," she urged again. When they came to a fork in the trail, someone had drawn an arrow in the dirt path, pointing which way they were to go. "This looks like the right direction," Sophie said, hurrying up the trail. "The others can't be that far ahead."

They made several turns in the trail before they finally caught up to Miss Rosy and their cabin mates. Miss Rosy had stopped in front of a tall, prickly bush. "Oh, there you two are," the counsellor said. "I was starting to worry. Now these are salmonberries, and they're delicious if you can find ripe ones."

Sophie nodded, trying to catch her breath.

"They're so yummy," Betty said. "Especially these purple ones."

"I've had them before," Brenda said. "They taste a bit like raspberries. You should try one, Elizabeth."

Elizabeth wrinkled her nose. "No thanks. They might have a worm or something inside."

"Yuck!" Margaret said, spitting out the one she had just popped into her mouth.

But Ginette loved the berries. The girl couldn't get enough. She picked them by the handful and crammed them into her mouth until purple juice dribbled down her chin.

Sophie noticed Elizabeth and Margaret exchanging disgusted looks. Why did Ginette have to do things like that?

"We mustn't get too spread out, so let's try to catch up to the other cabins. Come on," Miss Rosy urged, starting up the path again.

"Let's go, Ginette!" Sophie demanded. "I'm not getting behind again."

Ginette left the salmonberries reluctantly, wiping her juicy chin with the back of her hand. As they continued hiking up the hill, the path became steeper and narrower. They came to a muddy section around which they had to detour in single file.

Margaret asked in a whiny voice, "When will we get to the lake? I'm tired."

"We're about halfway there," Miss Rosy said.

"Only halfway!" Elizabeth wailed. "My feet are aching and so are my legs."

Miss Rosy started singing, "Oh, it's a long way to Tipperary. It's a long way to go..."

Sophie was still at the end of the line, but she joined in the singing with her loud voice. If there were any bears around, they would definitely head the other way. When Miss Rosy finished the song, Sophie sang out, "I love to go a-wandering."

Miss Rosy began singing, too, and soon all the girls were chiming in with "Valleree, Vallerah..."

After a while, Sophie felt too hot, so she took off her jacket and tied it around her waist by the sleeves. But then the strings from the heavy bag of oranges dug into her shoulder, so she had to carry it in her hand.

Ginette was holding her drawstring bag in her hand, as well. In fact, her whole hand was *in* the bag. And she was chewing!

"Sacré bleu, Ginette!" Sophie hissed. "You're not eating that banana loaf, are you?"

Ginette pulled her hand out of the bag and hid it behind her back. She stopped chewing.

"That loaf was to share with everyone," Sophie whispered. "You're supposed to be carrying it, not eating it!"

Ginette swallowed hard and stared at the ground guiltily. *"J'ai faim.* So hungry," she mumbled.

"We'll be there soon and having lunch. You have to wait, just like everyone else. Here, I'd better carry that banana loaf or there'll be none left by the time we get to the end of the trail." She took the canvas bag from Ginette. Now she had two bags to carry. The oranges and the banana bread. Plus her towel. She slung one bag over each shoulder. "Here, take my towel," she told Ginette. "At least you can't eat that."

Frowning, Ginette put Sophie's towel over her shoulders.

Although the sun was behind the clouds, Sophie felt hot and sticky. Her back was wet, and sweat trickled down her sides. She was just thinking about taking off her sweater when the hikers stopped.

"Finally we're here," Elizabeth said, panting. Her cheeks were as red as her hair ribbon.

"Almost," Miss Rosy said. "The lake is just around the next corner. But first I want to show you this magnificent view."

From the edge of the trail they could see right down the mountain, over the deep green treetops, all the way to the sea.

"Wow!" Peggy said. "Are those the islets we passed on our way to camp? They sure look small from here."

"Right. And way across the water," Miss Rosy said, pointing, "is Howe Sound. And that's Porteau Cove where we boarded the boat yesterday."

"Porteau?" Ginette asked.

"Yes, Porteau Cove. See, it's not that far at all."

Ginette nodded and stared hard at the cove and the misty north shore mountains behind it. Her pale eyes glittered.

As they hiked the rest of the way, the girls all sang, "Oh, we're here because we're here, because we're here."

Sophie sang, as well, but she was sure glad to get to the lake. The strings from the load of oranges were digging into her shoulder like knife blades.

"Who wants to go for a dip in the lake before lunch?" Miss Rosy called out.

"Me! I do!" Sophie cried with the rest of the girls. She dropped the drawstring bags on the pile of food near a log and pulled off her sweater, shorts, and shoes, then followed the other girls along the short dirt path to the lake. It was a small lake of brownish water surrounded by water plants, ferns, and overhanging trees. The girls from the other two cabins were already in the water, splashing and shrieking.

"*Eeou!*" Elizabeth squealed. "The bottom's all muddy and squishy!"

"*Eeou!*" Margaret echoed her. "There are probably leeches!"

Miss Rosy said, "No, there aren't any leeches. Don't be such scaredy-cats, you two."

"We can go this way," Sophie said, balancing her way along an evergreen tree that had fallen into the water near the lake's edge. She tiptoed along the broad trunk, holding out her arms like a tightrope walker. The bark was rough under her feet. When she came to the bushy crown of the tree, she took a quick breath, held her nose, and leaped into the water. It splashed up around her, surprisingly warm. She bobbed to the surface and yelled, "Come on in, you guys. The water's great!" She floated on her back and gazed up at the sky. Puffy white clouds skidded across.

Betty and Brenda soon followed her.

"Just a minute, Sophie!" Miss Rosy called out. "Come back here, please. I want to talk to you."

Sophie pulled herself back up onto the tree trunk and returned to shore.

"Did you forget you're supposed to stay with your buddy, Sophie?"

"But Ginette doesn't want to go swimming. She never does. Can't I swim with Brenda and Betty?"

"I guess so. Ginette, you stay here with the picnic. You can look after it for us," Miss Rosy told her.

Sophie didn't think it was such a great idea to put Ginette in charge of the lunch. She would probably eat the whole banana loaf and anything else she could get her hands on. But Sophie wanted so badly to go for a swim in that lovely water that she merely shrugged and headed back to the lake.

At the edge of the water both Elizabeth and Margaret were still squealing about mud and leeches, but Betty and Brenda loved swimming in the warm water as much as Sophie did. They took turns jumping off the end of the tree trunk and splashing around. Sophie floated on her back. Yes! This was what camp was all about!

After a while, Miss Rosy cried out, "Lunchtime, everyone! Come on in. Let's have our picnic. I'm starving."

Sophie followed Brenda and Betty back along the tree truck to the log where they had put their extra clothes and the food.

"Two of these big buttered buns and a hard-boiled egg each," Miss Rosy said, passing around the food. "Yum! So delicious! And nutritious!"

Sophie agreed. She pulled her towel around her back and took a giant bite of her egg sandwich. Delicious, all right. She hadn't realized how famished she was until she started eating.

Miss Rosy handed out the oranges. "And don't forget to drink plenty of water," she said, pouring water from the canteens into their tin cups. "Now for our dessert. Mrs. Carson's famous banana loaf. What a treat! Hmm. Where is it? Has anyone seen the banana loaf?"

Sophie caught her breath as everyone searched under the mound of towels and clothes for the banana loaf. Ginette sat there with the hood of her yellow raincoat pulled over her head and her hands behind her back. She seemed very uncomfortable.

"Here it is!" Peggy pounced and grabbed the drawstring bag from behind Ginette. She peered into the bag. "What's left of it, anyway," she said, dumping out the rest of the loaf.

Sophie was so embarrassed that she didn't know where to look. Ginette had eaten almost half the big loaf!

"What do you expect from a dumb DP, anyway?" Margaret snorted.

"Margaret, that was very unkind!" Miss Rosy scolded. "We don't call people names. I want you to apologize."

Margaret was mad, but she muttered, "Sorry," to Ginette, her lips barely moving.

Ginette didn't look up from the ground.

Disappointed, Miss Rosy said, "Oh, Ginette, the banana loaf was to share with everyone."

Ginette pulled her hood tighter and kept her eyes lowered.

"Well, there's still enough for a slice each," Miss Rosy said, opening her pocketknife. She cut the rest of the loaf into thin slices and passed them around.

"No thanks," Sophie said. She couldn't take any. The girls probably thought that it was just as much her fault as Ginette's.

EIGHT

On their way back down the mountain, Sophie made sure to stay close to her cabin mates. She hurried Ginette along. They were about halfway down, near the place they had stopped to pick salmonberries, when Miss Rosy halted abruptly.

"Hey!" she shouted. "Get out! Get out of here!" She clapped loudly. "It's a bear! Make as much noise as you can, girls!"

Sophie's heart throbbed in her throat. She joined the other girls, yelling and clapping. "Get out of here, bear! Go away!" She picked up a stick and slashed the bushes. "Go away!"

There was a sudden rustle, and a dark, shadowy shape scampered deep into the bushes. *Must be the escaping bear,* Sophie thought. She yelled even louder.

"That's it, girls!" Miss Rosy said. "He's gone now. We scared him off. Well done! Oh, watch out. Don't step in that." She pointed at a round plop on the ground beside the salmonberry bushes.

"What's that?" Margaret asked.

"Bear scat," Miss Rosy said.

"What's scat?"

"You know. His droppings."

"Eeou!" Margaret squealed, and so did all the other girls.

"Let's hurry and get back to camp," Miss Rosy told them. "And everyone sing as loud as you can."

"We'll be coming round the mountain when we come," Sophie shouted out with her cabin mates.

When they got back down the mountain to camp, everything was in an uproar.

"Where's Danny?" Mrs. Carson asked. "He's missing! No one's seen him since breakfast. Have you girls seen him?"

Sophie gulped. The glimpse of red she had seen flashed through her mind. Maybe Danny had tried to follow them and got lost in the woods. He could be anywhere. The bear! She gulped again. Should she say something?

"Such a cute little guy!" one girl said.

"What if that bear got him?" Peggy said, her eyes huge.

"Bear?" Miss Bottomly asked.

"We think we might have seen a bear on our way down the mountain," Miss Rosy told her.

"Oh, dear!" Miss Bottomly said, her hand over her mouth.

People began dashing all over the place.

Miss Bottomly clapped her hands for everyone's attention. "Girls," she said in her loud, stern voice, "stop this instant. There's no point getting into a panic."

Everyone froze to listen to her.

"Let's have a plan," Miss Bottomly went on. "First, and let me emphasize this, stay with your buddy. Especially now. Girls from cabins one and two, I want you to check the beach area and around the mess hall. Girls from cabin three, check all the cabins, including under all the beds. Danny may have crawled under one of the bunks and fallen asleep. And girls from cabins four and five, you have the toughest job. I want you to search the woods along the trail from here to the lake. Everyone report back to the flagpole in one hour at five o'clock. If we do find Danny, we'll ring the bell. Again, please stay with your counsellors, your cabin mates, and your buddies at all times. Hurry now."

The girls and their counsellors dispersed. The girls from cabin four turned around and headed back up the lake trail, following Miss Rosy. Sophie was right behind her.

"I have an idea," Sophie said to the counsellor.

"What is it?"

"I'm not sure, but I think Danny might have started to follow us when we were going up to the lake."

"Did you see him?"

"Well, not exactly. Not really. I noticed a flash of red when we turned onto the trail."

"And you didn't say anything?"

"I know I should have, but you guys were way up ahead, so we had to catch up. And then...and then I just forgot about it, I guess."

"Oh, Sophie! What if Danny did try to follow you and got lost in these woods? He could be anywhere. There are miles and miles of trails in these woods. And that bear..."

Sophie didn't know what to say. She had a big lump in her throat and fought back tears. She could barely swallow. "Maybe he turned left at the fork where we went right?" she suggested.

"Come on, girls," Miss Rosy said. "We've got to hurry. It looks like the girls from cabin five are going straight up to the lake, so let's try this lower trail first. And keep making plenty of noise."

The girls got long sticks and rushed along the trail. They poked into the underbrush and ferns to search. "Danny!" they called loudly. "Danny! Where are you?"

Sophie's heart beat frantically. She shouted until her throat ached. If that bear got Danny, it would be all her fault. She slashed at the bushes and yelled even louder.

"Gently now," Miss Rosy cautioned. "We wouldn't want to hurt him if he was in there."

They checked all the underbrush between their cabin and the start of the lake trail, but found nothing. Sophie felt more and more panicky by the minute.

"Let's try this trail," Miss Rosy said. "Be sure to keep together, no matter what."

It wasn't long before Ginette let out a gasp and tugged at Sophie's arm. "Sophie! *Regardes!* Look!" she squeaked, pointing at a patch of red under a thick bush.

Sophie pushed through the underbrush and stared. Danny! He was curled into a ball behind a moss-covered rock, fast asleep. She breathed deeply and grinned at Ginette. "Miss Rosy!" she cried out. "We found him! Ginette found Danny! He's right here! And he's okay. The bear didn't get him."

Everyone rushed over and peered into the bush.

Danny stirred at the sound of their voices, then opened his eyes. He nearly jumped when he saw everyone gaping at him.

"Hi, Danny," Sophie said quietly, bending down. "We're sure glad we found you."

Danny looked disappointed. "I thought this was the best hiding spot ever."

"It was a great hiding place, Danny," Miss Rosy said, brushing the dirt and twigs off his red shirt and pants and from his curly hair. She gave him a big hug. "It was too good. You gave us all a terrible scare. We thought you were lost."

He shook his head. "Me? I'd never get lost. But I sure am hungry. When's lunch?"

The girls all laughed.

"Hey, want a shoulder ride back to the mess hall?" Sophie offered.

Danny nodded enthusiastically as Sophie stooped. He climbed onto her shoulders, and she carried him down the trail to camp.

When Mrs. Carson saw them coming, she ran up to Sophie. "Danny! Danny!" she shouted. When Sophie let him down from her shoulders, Mrs. Carson scooped him up, not knowing whether to hug him or scold him, so she did both at the same time.

Supper of fried chicken and baked potatoes and chocolate cake for dessert was a bit late that evening, but when it came, everyone enjoyed it all the more. Especially Sophie. But the best part, besides finding Danny safe, was that everyone seemed to have forgotten that Ginette had been such a hog and had eaten most of the banana loaf.

That night the girls in cabin four took forever to settle down. It had started raining again, and the wind was howling among the tall, swaying trees, but the bunks in the cabins were cozy and warm.

"Go to sleep, you guys," Miss Rosy begged for about the fifth time. "I'm exhausted. Please, please, please, go to sleep! Okay, the next person to make a sound will be stuck outside in the rain."

That shut the girls up, except for a bit of giggling. But soon even the giggling stopped, and all Sophie could hear was the rain swishing against the roof and the windows rattling in their frames. She tossed in her bunk and tried to find a comfortable spot for her head on the towel-covered flashlight that was her lumpy pillow. Finally she fell into a deep sleep.

After a long time, the bunk moved, jolting Sophie awake. It took her a few seconds to realize it was Ginette climbing down the ladder from the upper bunk. The cabin door squeaked open and clicked closed.

She must be going to the washroom, Sophie thought. She turned her face to the wall and curled her legs, but she couldn't get back to sleep. The whole cabin was totally dark, and except for someone snoring softly in the bunk across the room from her, and the wind blowing rain against the roof, it was silent.

Sophie sighed deeply and pulled her blanket around her back more tightly. She held her breath and waited for Ginette to return, but she didn't.

Maybe the girl had taken the wrong path and got lost. It was so dark and stormy out there. She probably didn't even have a flashlight. Sophie thought she'd better check on Ginette. Besides, now she had to go to the bathroom, too.

Sophie grabbed her rain jacket and shuffled into her running shoes. She fished out her flashlight from inside her towel and tiptoed to the door. Silently she opened it, went out, and shut it with a quiet click. Now she was glad Maman had insisted that she take her warm flannelette nightgown, even though it was decorated with dancing reindeers and came only to her knees.

She pulled her jacket hood over her head and started down the path to the washroom, following a wet tunnel of raindrops lit by her flashlight. The wind had picked up and was moaning through the tall evergreen trees. Sophie had to hold on to her hood to keep it on. She squinted as cold raindrops blew into her face.

A single oil lamp, swaying slightly from the ceiling above the row of sinks, illuminated the washroom and cast shifting shadows along the concrete floor. "Ginette? Are you here?" Sophie whispered loudly into the dimness.

No answer.

She checked the toilet cubicles, but Ginette wasn't there.

Strange, Sophie thought. After using the toilet, she left the cabin and searched outside. A movement down at the dock caught her eye. That was odd. Someone was on the dock near the canoes. Sophie hurried down. As she ran, she saw that the wind had blown up the water in the cove into pale frothy whitecaps.

Sophie tore down the path to the slick ramp, tripping once and skinning her knee. Someone was in a canoe and paddling toward open water! "Ginette, is that you?" she nearly yelled. She flashed her flashlight and captured a glimpse of yellow. Ginette's yellow rain jacket! And she wasn't wearing a life preserver! Waves buffeted the boat, but Ginette was paddling determinedly away from the dock.

"Ginette! Where do you think you're going? Come back here right now!" Sophie demanded. Ginette didn't even glance around. She kept her head low and paddled away, picking up speed, the bow of the canoe slicing through the waves.

Sophie hesitated. Should she run and tell Miss Rosy? Wake up everyone? They would both get into such terrible trouble if Miss Bottomly found out. They'd probably lose about a thousand points. Maybe they'd even be sent home!

Sophie slid down the steep ramp to the dock. She would have to get Ginette back herself. "Ginette! Come back here!"

Ginette continued paddling.

Sophie rushed to the pile of life preservers. She had to watch her step because the wet boards on the dock were so slippery. She seized one of the life preservers, pulled it over her head, and fumbled with the ties, then took a deep breath. The life preserver gave her courage. It was like tying on a Star Girl cape.

She had to get a life preserver out to Ginette. The girl's canoe could easily capsize in the wind. Sophie had to get her back. What did she think she was doing? Where could Ginette be going? Should she wake up Miss Rosy? By the time she got here, though, it might be too late. Ginette's canoe might have tipped over by then, and without a life preserver...

"A Star Girl rescue," Sophie announced out loud. "That's what's needed here. I'll convince Ginette to come back. She's such a little kid, I should be able to catch up with her in no time at all."

NINE

Sophie grabbed another life preserver and a paddle and untied the closest canoe, which was bouncing against the dock. Gingerly she stepped into the centre of the boat, pushed off from the dock with her paddle, and began paddling for all she was worth. The canoe bounced up with every wave, but Sophie stroked as hard as she could, digging into the waves, first on one side, then on the other, trying to keep the boat going in a straight line.

"Come on, Star Girl!" she panted. "Come on!"

Although she was kneeling on the bottom of the canoe, it felt really tippy in the choppy water. She figured this must be what it was like on the back of a galloping horse. You could be bucked off at any moment.

It didn't take long to paddle out of the calmer area of the sheltered cove. But as the boat rounded the point, the wind and rain struck her with full force. The storm was so much wilder out here. It blew cold salt water onto her cheeks and lips, but she was hot inside her jacket. Hot with worry.

She squinted straight ahead at the back of Ginette's yellow jacket. Ginette wasn't following the edge of the island. She was heading straight out into Howe Sound. Straight out into the dark, stormy, and deep water. It looked as if she was heading back to Porteau Cove!

"Ginette! Don't be a goof!" Sophie yelled her loudest, now that she was away from the camp. "Come back here! Where are you going?"

But Ginette kept on paddling, not missing a single stroke. Not even glancing back at Sophie.

Sophie paddled her hardest, ploughing into the waves, but she wasn't gaining on Ginette at all. In fact, she seemed to be getting even farther away. Ginette could certainly paddle fast. They both paddled past rocks and reefs bashed by foaming waves.

Sophie had no idea what time it was, just that it was the middle of the night. Although clouds filled the sky, she could still see well enough to make out the whitecaps raging around her canoe. There was a lightness in the sky, as though the full moon was doing its best to shine through a thin bank of clouds.

Her shoulders and arms were aching, so she switched sides again, paddling on her left now. She breathed hard as she concentrated on steering the boat away from the rocks and keeping it upright.

"This is really, really stupid," she grumbled. "Stupid! Stupid!" She should have woken Miss Rosy and told her that Ginette was missing. But it was too late now. If she didn't get to Ginette on time, no one would. And it would be all her fault.

The rain and wind were still strong, but they were mostly at her back now. As she dug into the water with her paddle, she felt as if she were almost flying from frothy wave tip to wave tip. But she still wasn't gaining on Ginette. She paddled for quite a long time, following Ginette out into the open water, keeping her eyes on the yellow coat and paddling her hardest. "Come on, Star Girl. You can do it! Come on. Come on," she kept muttering to herself.

Suddenly Ginette wasn't there! She had vanished!

"Oh, my gosh!" Sophie said out loud frantically. But then she spotted Ginette in the water. A wave had swamped her canoe, and now only the front tip of the boat was above water. It was sinking fast! Ginette struggled to stay afloat, slashing at the waves with one hand and clinging to the sinking canoe's bow with the other, her eyes dark with terror in an ash-white face.

Desperately Sophie paddled as she had never paddled before. She finally reached Ginette just as the canoe sank into the waves.

"Here's a life preserver!" Sophie shouted, breathing hard as she threw it toward the girl.

Ginette snatched it and thrashed toward Sophie's boat.

"Come on, get in!" Sophie yelled as she paddled the canoe alongside Ginette.

Ginette's eyes were wild, her fair hair plastered to her head. She flailed around in the water and clutched at the side of the canoe. In a flash Sophie's canoe lurched, flipped over, and dumped her into the sea, as well.

"Sacré bleu!" she gasped as cold salt water rolled over her head. She swallowed a mouthful, but she bounced up to the surface like a cork, her life preserver snug around her neck. Sophie coughed and spat up water to clear her lungs and splashed toward the overturned canoe, grabbing at the hull. She didn't see Ginette anywhere. Her heart pounded.

"Ginette!" she screamed. "Ginette! Where are you?"

A wave rolled over her, and for a moment she couldn't see anything except blackness, but she bobbed back up to the surface again. She coughed some more, blew her nose, and rubbed her face, blinking hard to get the burning salt water out of her eyes. She was filled with terror.

"Ginette! Where are you!" she screamed again. She had never been so scared.

Then she saw Ginette clinging to the other side of the over-turned boat with one hand and clasping the life preserver with the other. Another wave tumbled over them. Sophie squeezed her eyes shut and hugged the canoe with all her strength. When she caught her breath, she yelled at Ginette, "That was stupid! Stupid! Stupid! Stupid!"

"Sorry," Ginette muttered. "So sorry. I not mean to make boat go over." There were tears in her husky voice.

"So now what can we do?" Sophie asked desperately.

Ginette just shook her head and clung to the overturned canoe and the life jacket, gasping for breath.

The water was so cold that Sophie's legs throbbed. Her whole body throbbed. She wriggled her toes to see if they were still there. They seemed to be. Her nightgown ballooned around her in the water. "Let's head for that islet," she yelled. "Kick hard. We'll get there. Push the boat. Turn it right side up. Empty it somehow. Just hope it stays afloat."

Ginette nodded. She held on to her side of the canoe and kicked hard. Sophie kicked hard, too, her running shoes splashing behind her. She kept her eyes on the small rocky island jutting out of the waves. At first it looked as if they weren't making any head-way at all, but eventually the island seemed a little closer. Ginette stopped kicking.

"Come on, Ginette, we're almost there," Sophie cried, panting. "Don't stop! Kick! Kick!"

Ginette began kicking again.

The overturned canoe was very awkward to push through the water. After what felt like hours, the boat banged against the rocks. Waves were splashing onto them. Sophie let go of the boat and clutched at the rocks. Ginette did, too.

Sophie took a big breath of relief. The rocks were wet and cold, but they felt solid and safe. "We made it," she muttered. "Oh, no!" she yelled as a wave pulled the boat away. "The boat! Grab it! Grab the canoe!"

Sophie splashed after the boat, but it was too late. The current pulled the canoe away from the islet and out of her reach. She thrashed her way back, grasped a rounded rock, and pulled herself up onto it. It was smooth except for a few barnacles and shells and slimy seaweed. She reached down for Ginette's hand and helped her scramble out of the water and up onto the rocks, as well. Then she scanned the dark water for the boat, but it was gone. Vanished without a trace.

"The boat's gone. What are we going to do?" Sophie swallowed back sobs, her voice sounding hoarse and broken.

Ginette didn't answer. She was huddled on the rock, her thin arms hugging her life preserver, her pale wet hair plastered against her scalp. She was shivering really hard.

Sophie was trembling with cold, too. She pulled her jacket and sodden nightgown down over her knees and rubbed her eyes, then took another big breath. At least they were both out of the water, she told herself. She rocked back and forth, clasping her knees tightly, trying to stop shivering.

Ginette opened her pale, smouldering eyes and stared at Sophie. "Why you came after me?"

"What? I had to. You're my buddy, my responsibility, remember? Why did you leave camp? Getting into that canoe in this storm in the middle of the night is about the stupidest thing I've ever heard of. Especially without a life preserver. You could have drowned out there!"

Ginette shrugged and looked out at the wind-whipped waves.

"Don't you realize how dangerous it was?" Sophie asked.

Ginette shook her head. "Not so dangerous. I have the dreidel."

"Dreidel?"

Ginette fished a string from her shirt. It was hard to see in the dim light what dangled from the string, but it appeared to be a small four-sided toy.

"What's so special about that?" Sophie asked. "Looks like a stupid wooden top to me."

"Not stupid. Very special. My papa made it and it keep us safe."

Sophie shook her head. "Just because you have some lucky charm from your father, doesn't mean it will save you when you do something stupid and dangerous. You were just lucky you didn't drown. Anyway, we've got to get back to camp. Any ideas?"

Ginette shook her head and continued staring out at the dark water.

"I sure hope the tide isn't rising," Sophie said. "If it is, we're in trouble. This whole islet will be covered with water pretty soon."

Each bank of waves that rolled toward the rocks seemed higher and higher. Now the waves were licking greedily at Sophie's wet shoes. She pulled them under her and shifted uneasily to a higher rock, staring at the water and willing it to stop rising.

TEN

"Porteau," Ginette mumbled. "I go to Porteau."

"Porteau? That's where you were heading?"

Ginette nodded.

"But why? Even on a calm day that would be a long paddle from the camp. And dangerous, too. It would take you hours to get there in a canoe. And there's nothing at Porteau. Just a bunch of boats."

"Have to go Vancouver."

"Vancouver? Why? We'll all be going back home at the end of the week. That's only five days away."

"My sister," Ginette blurted out, "*ma petite soeur*. My little sister..."

"What about your sister?"

"She small, only seven years, and her ears, she not hear so good. Just me. She hear when I talk very slow right in her face."

"But what about your mom and dad?"

Ginette shook her head. "Papa, he killed in war fighting in the underground for *la Belle France*. Five, six years now," she said flatly. "And Maman, she not found yet. Maybe she dead, too."

"But who looks after you? Who do you live with?"

"We have auntie. *Ma tante Lise*. But she sad. Sometime she not get up from her bed. She even sadder than when we live in refugee camp. So Selina, little sister, I look after her. Only me."

"I have a little brother," Sophie said, nodding. "And sometimes when Maman is busy I have to look after him."

"Last week big, loud bang came *à la porte*," Ginette said. "I not open it. Selina and me, we hide in closet. But after a while, landlady upstairs come down and unlock door and let in other lady. Social worker, she say, from Catholic Charities. She look all round kitchen. So big mess. Lots of dishes I not wash yet. Selina's shirt still wet where she spill tea, so social worker take her away. And she take me and Auntie Lise away, too. And now Selina, she not have dreidel. No sleeping. *Elle pleur*. She cry all the time."

"She wants the dreidel?"

Ginette nodded. "Selina always have it to sleep. I have to bring it to her. Papa tell me before he go away. Always stay with sister. I promise. For whole war, when we hide, in all the camps, I all the time stay with sister."

"But that's no reason to leave our camp in that little canoe in the middle of a storm," Sophie said.

"I have to leave here. They will put me in another camp again and...and..."

"And what?"

Ginette shut her eyes and shivered. "Camp too terrible..."

"What are you talking about? They're all nice here. Even Miss Bottomly isn't so bad."

Ginette shook her head and glanced at Sophie. "You think they all nice, but then they come for you in night and...and..." She shivered again, and her eyes filled with tears. She put her head on her arms. Sobs wracked her body as she rocked herself back and forth.

Sophie was dumbfounded. She had heard stories on the radio, terrible stories about what had happened to people in refugee camps and concentration camps during the war, and after, especially to Jewish people. But those awful things happened just to adults, not to little kids, didn't they?

She was beginning to understand why Ginette was so desperate to get away. Sophie rubbed the girl's back, trying to soothe away her sobs. Her back was so thin that Sophie could feel the sharp bones in her shoulders. Ginette soon stopped crying. She sniffed loudly and wiped her nose with the back of her hand.

"So how come you're here at this camp?" Sophie asked her.

Ginette sighed. "Social worker say I go to camp until they find good home and family for me. But I say I already have family. I try to get away, but they watch all the time. And Selina, they take her to special school, they say. I think maybe she here at this camp. So I come. But she not here."

"Look, Miss Bottomly, the camp leader really is nice. I bet if we talk to her she'll call the authorities and fix everything for you. She said that if anyone had any problems at all, just to go to her. She'll know what to do."

Ginette stared at Sophie with narrowed eyes. "You think she nice? I not think so. She just pretend."

"What about Miss Rosy? You must like her. She's really fun."

Ginette frowned. "Maybe Miss Rosy. Maybe not."

"Well, with no boat we can't go anywhere, anyway. We'll have to stay here until the morning. When Miss Rosy sees we're gone, they'll come out here and rescue us," Sophie said with more confidence than she felt. She didn't want to admit it, but the waves were definitely getting higher. "Come on. We'll have to move up to that rock now," she told Ginette.

They crawled up to the highest rock on the islet and crouched beside a short, thick log that sheltered them a bit from the wind. The other rocks that made up the small islet had disappeared under the rising tide. And the rock they were perched on was coated with barnacles and slimy seaweed, which probably meant it spent a lot of time underwater.

"Ginette," Sophie said quietly, "it looks like this whole islet will be underwater pretty soon. We'll have to leave it whether we want to or not."

Ginette gazed out across the water at the dark bulk that was Porteau Cove and the mainland. She fingered the dreidel.

"There's no way we can make it to Porteau," Sophie said. "So don't even think about it. But I bet we could make it back to Gambier."

"But my sister…"

"Look, when we get back to camp, I'll talk to Miss Bottomly for you. I'll ask her to find out where your sister is and make sure she gets the dreidel. We don't have a choice. The waves will soon cover this rock. We have to get back to the island, then make our way back to camp."

Ginette was quiet for a while, then said, "Maybe I go to island but not to camp."

Sophie nodded. If she could get Ginette back to the island, she would talk to her then and convince her to go back to camp. First things first, though. How in the world were they going to get from the rock to the island? It was way too far to swim.

Sophie looked around the rock they were perched on. There wasn't much left of it, and the bit that remained was disappearing fast under the lapping waves. She felt panic rise in her chest.

"Let's use this log," she said. "We can float on it like a raft and paddle it with our hands and feet. It shouldn't be that hard to get to shore." She knew she sounded a lot braver than she felt. Their tiny islet was growing smaller by the moment.

Ginette agreed reluctantly. She pulled her life preserver on and tied it tightly.

"Help me push the log into the water and then get on it," Sophie said. They hurriedly got behind the log and pushed. "Push harder," Sophie groaned.

The log was amazingly heavy. They grunted and heaved, and finally it rolled off the rock and into the water. A wave splashed against the log and threatened to carry it away, but Sophie leaped into the shallow water and grabbed it. Surprisingly the water didn't feel all that cold.

"Here, I'll hold the log steady while you get on," Sophie said.

Ginette climbed onto the log and straddled it, one leg on each side, as if it were a horse. Sophie hiked up her sodden nightgown and jumped onto the log behind Ginette. "Let's go!" she shouted.

They pushed the log into deeper water. It jolted as a wave hit it, but Sophie held on tight. It was like riding a bucking bronco. "Balance it! Balance!" Sophie cried.

"I can't!" Ginette squeaked.

The log rolled, and they both fell off, sputtering salt water.

"Grab it, grab it!" Sophie yelled as a big wave threatened to carry the log away.

They both lunged and caught it. Sophie wrapped her arm around the log, feeling defeated. What could they do? They were much too far from land to swim, even with life preservers on, especially with the sea so rough. Could Ginette even swim?

"We hold on to log and kick hard. Like canoe," Ginette said, her voice quavering.

"You're right," Sophie agreed, swallowing her fear. "We could push the log through the water! Thank goodness we've got these life preservers."

At first they tried pushing the log, both on the same side and kicking hard, but they didn't seem to get anywhere and they kept kicking each other.

"Hold on," Sophie said. "I'll move to the other side." She went around the back of the log. "Okay, let's try it again." She clasped the log with one hand, paddled through the water with the other, and kicked her feet as hard as she could.

Ginette did the same. Sophie soon felt warmer from the kicking. Or maybe she was just numb from the cold water. At least she wasn't shivering as much.

This was a lot harder than any Star Girl rescue Sophie had ever read about in her Star Girl comics. Panting, she kicked and paddled, fighting to keep her panic at bay.

On the other side of the log Ginette kicked and paddled, too, until she groaned. "Tired," she began muttering. "Too tired."

"Me, too," Sophie gasped. "Let's stop. Rest. Closer. We must be closer."

The wind was still howling and the waves were still crashing around them, but they held on to the log and managed to ride out most of the waves.

"That rock. Over there," Sophie panted, pointing at a rock whose top was barely visible above the waves. "Let's try. Get to that rock."

Ginette nodded and started kicking again.

Sophie kicked as hard as she could, but it seemed as if they would never get there. Her legs felt so heavy that it took all her effort to keep them moving. "Come on, Star Girl," she murmured to herself, forcing her legs through the water. "Come on, Star Girl!"

"Star Girl?" Ginette asked. "Who Star Girl?"

"I'll tell you," Sophie gasped, "when we get there. To that rock."

They kicked and paddled some more and finally they made it. Sophie inhaled deeply as the log bumped against the rock. The rock was too small to hold them both, but they could stand in the shallow water at its base and rest. Suddenly a big wave splashed over the rock and snatched away the log. Ginette leaped out and grabbed it, clinging to it with both hands.

"Good going, Ginette!" Sophie firmly held on to the other side of the log and took some deep breaths. A few minutes later she asked, "Think we can make it to shore now?"

Ginette shook her head. "Too far. Too tired."

"Star Girl wouldn't let a bit of water get her down," Sophie said.

"I don't know Star Girl. You say you tell me."

"Look, when we get to shore, I'll tell you everything I know about Star Girl. And that's plenty."

Ginette sighed heavily, and they pushed off the rock. Hugging the log, they kicked and paddled through the waves, the log bouncing between them. It felt as if hours passed, and Sophie's lungs burned. She kept kicking and kicking hard, though her legs ached to the bone and were as heavy as cement. They stopped more and more often for longer rests. Thankfully the wind was at their backs and gave them a much-needed push.

"We can make it, Ginette! We can make it! Just a little farther."

"Can't, Sophie. Can't. Too tired," Ginette spluttered, shaking her head. Her arm slipped from the log.

"Ginette!" Sophie shouted, struggling to the other side of the log and catching Ginette before she floated away. She pulled the girl near the log and lifted her arm. "Here. Put your hand here. Hang on. I'll do the kicking. Just hang on!"

Ginette's eyes closed and her head fell forward.

"You *have* to!" Sophie screamed in her ear and squeezed her arm. "You just have to! Think about your little sister! Think about Selina! Come on. Don't give up now! Please, Ginette. Let's count." Sophie counted in time with her stroking through the water. "One, two, three. Count, Ginette!"

Ginette halfheartedly counted, too, her lips barely moving. Slowly she began kicking again. When they got to one hundred, Sophie looked up. The island didn't look any closer.

"Frère Jacques, Frère Jacques," Sophie panted as she kicked.

Ginette joined her, mumbling at first in a tired, whispery voice, then louder and louder. Unexpectedly Ginette started singing "Au Claire de la Lune" and kicked in time with that.

Relief flooded Sophie as she realized Ginette was really trying. They sang the song more than twenty times, over and over again. "Papa's favourite song," Sophie gasped. "Always sings it. Big loud voice."

"My papa sing, too," Ginette murmured. "He throw me up in air, all the time up in air." Her voice sounded so wistful and far away that Sophie was afraid she was falling asleep.

"Let's sing it again, Ginette. Come on! Really loud. For our papas. *Au claire de la lune, mon ami...* Oh, look!" she cried. "We're almost there! We're almost at the island!"

When Sophie glanced up this time, the dark bulk of the island filled her eyes, cutting out the luminous sky. She kicked at the water with renewed vigour. She felt Ginette kicking harder, too. Were they really going to make it?

Eventually the waves and wind drove their log against the shore. Sophie let go and crawled up onto the rocks. They were slippery with rain and seaweed and sharp with barnacles, but they felt so good and solid under her elbows and fingers and knees that she felt like kissing them.

"We're here, Ginette. We made it! We're safe!"

Ginette was a few feet away, clinging to the rocks, half lying in the water.

"Come on. Climb up onto these rocks. You can do it," Sophie encouraged. "Get right out of the water."

Ginette nodded but didn't move. She seemed to have given up. Her eyes fluttered closed.

Sophie scrambled over the rocks and back into the water. Grunting, she pushed Ginette higher onto the rocks, above the rising tide. Then Sophie crawled up beside the girl, and with the last of her strength, she dragged them both up the steep bank a little higher so they would be out of reach of the waves and spray.

She felt as if a huge weight were pressing down on her shoulders and back. Even blinking was too much effort. Her eyes closed and she drifted off to sleep, sprawled out on the rocky cliff.

ELEVEN

Sophie descended into sleep like a fish drifting down into a dark sea. Like the fish, she swirled around in the water of sleep, sailing up to the surface occasionally, aware of distant waves crashing before she floated back down into the dark water.

She woke suddenly. Was it minutes or hours later? She blinked and heard loud waves smashing against the cliff below her feet. Her head felt so heavy that she could barely lift it. Her neck was sore and her back ached. Above her, trees and bushes swayed in the wind. She turned her head. Close by, Ginette was curled into a ball, her eyes closed and her fingers entwined in string, clasping the dreidel tightly.

Shivering hard, Sophie sat up and crossed her arms over her knees, hugging herself tightly and rocking back and forth, trying to warm up. With the immediate threat of the ocean gone, she shuddered at the thought of the trek back to camp. She looked around, tugging her jacket closer to her neck and pulling the hem of her nightgown over her feet. The nightgown was soaked, but it sheltered her bare legs from the wind-driven rain. The sky seemed to be getting lighter, and the waves became silvery-coloured as they crashed and sprayed against the rocks.

Ginette's eyelids fluttered, and she opened her eyes. When she saw Sophie staring at her, she gasped and cringed.

"It's okay, Ginette." Sophie reached over and patted the girl's arm. "It's only me. Sophie. We're safe. We're going to be okay. We're both going to be just fine."

Ginette blinked, then took a deep, ragged breath and let it out slowly as she nodded. "I forget. For minute, I forget."

"I don't know how long we've been here," Sophie said. "But I think it's getting a little lighter out. I wonder what time it is."

Ginette glanced around at the narrow band of rocks between the sea and the trees behind them. In some places thick bushes grew down almost to the waterline.

"I think the wind's died down," Sophie said hopefully. She tried to give Ginette an encouraging smile.

Ginette was shivering, too. She pulled her coat tighter around her back. "Where is camp?"

"I think it must be that way," Sophie said, pointing to their left. "It can't be that far. Maybe it's just around that next point."

Ginette looked to their right. A steep and impenetrable rocky cliff loomed high above them.

Although it was still dark, Sophie could tell where the land was and where the water and the sky were. The land was a different sort of darkness—heavier, denser—than either the water or the sky. She opened her eyes as wide as she could and longed to open them even wider, so she could see better.

Ginette wiggled her bare toes.

"Where are your shoes?" Sophie asked.

"They come off in water."

Sophie sighed. "It's going to be really hard to walk barefoot on these rocks. They're so rough with all the barnacles."

Ginette hunched and held her feet in her hands as if to warm them.

"We should start moving," Sophie said. "If we could get back to camp and sneak into our bunks before anyone wakes up and finds us gone, that would be the best thing. Besides, if we don't move soon, we'll probably freeze to death in these wet clothes. I bet it's not that far back to camp."

Ginette shook her head. "Not going to camp," she said, her bottom lip quivering.

"What? Why not?"

Ginette shook her head again.

"That's crazy!" Sophie said. "You can't stay out here. There'll be nothing but a frozen icicle left of you in the morning."

Ginette folded her arms and stared straight ahead, blinking back tears.

"Come on, Ginette. I'll help you."

Ginette continued shaking her head.

"Fine," Sophie said. "I don't care. I'm heading back to camp. I can't wait to have a long, hot shower and get into some warm, dry clothes. Now that would be so lovely. We'll be so warm back in our beds. And for breakfast, I bet they'll be having something really delicious. Lovely hot cocoa, maybe even pancakes, or something yummy like that." She tried to make it sound as enticing as she could.

Ginette didn't move. Her chin was on her knees, and she continued to gaze at the dark water.

Finally Sophie sighed and said, "Well, see you later then." She edged her way slowly along the rocky cliff, then turned to look at Ginette. The girl was still sitting there, hugging her bare legs, lost and unhappy.

Sophie felt so sorry for her. She hesitated. Should she go back and try to convince her to come along? She breathed deeply. She had tried as hard as she could. It was no use. She turned away and kept going. Her wet nightgown flapped against her knees. She tried wringing out the hem, but it didn't help much. Her life preserver was stiff and uncomfortable, but she didn't dare take it off. It was the only thing keeping her neck and shoulders warm.

She studied the bank of bushes and trees above the cliffs. Would it be easier to go through the bush or along the cliff closer to the water's edge? She climbed up the cliff's steep face on her hands and knees to get a closer look. The bush at the top of the cliff was as dense as a solid wall and prickly with thorns. She couldn't see a way through it at all. It would be easier to find a route along the rocky cliff, she decided.

"Sophie! Wait!" Ginette called up to her.

Sophie smiled with relief and turned back. "We can't make it through this bush. It's way too thick," she said as Ginette worked her way up the cliff barefoot.

Sophie could almost feel the pain of the sharp rocks and barnacles cutting into Ginette's feet. She wanted to tell the girl how glad she was for the change of mind, but she couldn't think of how to say it. Instead, she reached down and helped her up to the top of the cliff, grinning at her. A faint smile crossed Ginette's face.

They continued along the cliff together, gradually finding their way over the rocks, some of them as big as cars, some even as large as houses. Ginette stepped carefully in her bare feet, but she didn't complain. They rounded another corner.

Ginette stopped suddenly in front of Sophie. "Now where we go?"

Sophie surveyed the steep face of the cliff in front of them. It was daunting. There was nothing to grip. The cliff plunged straight into the water. It was far too steep to climb across.

"We'll have to go up to the top of the cliff and climb over it that way somehow," Sophie said resolutely.

She led the way to the top of the cliff, clutching at roots and branches to help her climb. Thick bush grew right to the edge of the cliff, even overhanging it in some places, making the climb very tricky. She tried to push through the bush, but sharp thorns clawed at her face, arms, and legs. It was impassable.

"We can't get through here," she told Ginette. "The bush is way too thick."

Ginette didn't say anything.

Discouragement swept over Sophie as she contemplated the waves crashing against the rocks at the bottom of the steep cliff. "Looks like we'll have to get a little wet again. We'll have to swim across to the other side of the cliff."

"Go back into water? No," Ginette said, shaking her head. "I not go back into water. Too, too cold." She shivered.

"There's no other way. It's not that far across the bottom of the cliff. We swam a lot farther before. Look, once we get around that rock we can hold on to the edge of the cliff near the water and climb up there. It's not so far. Really," Sophie cajoled. Why did Ginette have to be so darn stubborn?

Ginette was still shaking her head and staring at the waves.

"Come on, Ginette," Sophie insisted, climbing down the steep cliff. "This is the only way and we are going."

Ginette didn't make any move to come down from the top of the cliff. She sat on the edge of a big rock, clasping her knees and frowning.

Finally Sophie said, "Fine, then. I'm going. You can stay up there all night and freeze for all I care." Star Girl had never had such a hard rescue. All the people she ever rescued *wanted* to be rescued. They were *grateful* to be rescued.

89

Sophie picked her way to the bottom of the cliff and around another big rock at the water's edge. She eased herself feet first into the water, gasping as it splashed up around her waist. It felt much colder than earlier. But she gritted her teeth, pushed herself off the rock, and paddled toward the cliff. The cold water ballooned her nightgown and pushed her life preserver snugly against her chin and cheeks. She trembled as the icy water seeped inside her jacket, up her back, and under her arms. She resolved to keep going, kicking and splashing hard, staying close to the edge.

At last she reached the overhanging cliff and glanced back at Ginette, who had crept down the cliff and was about to follow her into the water. A big wave crashed at the bottom of the cliff between them, and Ginette shrieked.

"Hold on to that root. It's tough," Sophie said, pushing herself back through the waves to help Ginette.

Ginette squealed again as Sophie gripped her hand and led her into the water.

"It's not that far across, Ginette. Come on. Hold on. I'll help you. There. You can do it. I know you can do it."

Ginette's pale eyes glittered with fear, but her mouth was determined as she pushed herself through the water, hand over hand, kicking her bare feet.

"Here's another place you can grab," Sophie told her. "And another one here."

Gradually they made their way in the water across the bottom of the steep cliff face.

"Hang on, Ginette!" Sophie cried. "Here comes another big wave." As the wave hit their backs and swept over their heads, she grasped a thick root with one hand and the back of Ginette's life preserver with the other. Ginette screamed and closed her eyes tight. Sophie shut her eyes, too. Then, in a panic, she felt the current tugging at them, pulling them back into the sea.

"Hold on tight, Ginette! Hold on! Don't let go!" Sophie's fingers clawed at the rocks as she fought with all her strength against the undertow.

The next wave was smaller, but the undertow yanked at them, trying to wrench them away from the cliff and back into the sea. They gripped the rocks and roots harder.

"Okay. The sea's a bit calmer. Let's move fast before another wave comes!" Sophie pushed through the water again, hand over hand, kicking her feet for momentum. Ginette followed her, and slowly they made their way across the bottom of the rock face to a shallow shelf.

"Good," Sophie grunted. "Let's climb out here and get onto the cliff. See, it's not so steep now."

But before they were able to pull themselves out of the water onto the shallow shelf, another wave engulfed them.

Quick!" Sophie yelled. "Grab that root before the undertow pulls us back in! The root!" With all her strength she pushed Ginette up onto the rocks.

Water streaming from her clothes, Ginette grabbed the root and scrambled up onto the shelf. She reached down and caught Sophie's hand. Sophie held on and dug into the cliff with her fingernails, trying to crawl up after Ginette on her hands and knees. But another big wave caught her. As it crashed over her back, she sucked in her breath and hung on for dear life, waiting for it to recede.

"Hurry, Sophie, climb now!" Ginette shouted.

In a brief moment of calm Sophie managed to pull herself out of the water and crawl up beside Ginette.

"Good, good," Ginette muttered, patting her arm.

They both stared down at the waves crashing against the cliff.

Sophie gasped until she caught her breath. "Thanks for giving me a hand. Wow, that was a close one."

Ginette shrugged.

"But we made it," Sophie said. "The rocks aren't so steep here. We could climb across it now."

She tried standing on the rocks, but her knees shook so badly that she had to hold on to a nearby root for support. Cold water streamed down her trembling legs. She wrung out the hem of her nightgown again and took a deep breath. "Let's go." Still shaking, she led the way, scrabbling over the rocks, trying to find a path that wouldn't be too hard on Ginette's bare feet. They both shivered violently. The rain and wind still blew strongly enough to pull the hood off Sophie's wet hair.

She climbed around one big rock that jutted out sharply. The other side of the rock seemed to fall away quite abruptly as if there was a large hollow in the rock face. Sophie followed the contours, feeling the edge with her fingertips, and suddenly the wind stopped. She opened her eyes as widely as she could and gazed straight ahead, but saw only darkness.

"A cave!" she said, waving her hands around. "Hey, Ginette, we've found a cave!"

"Cave?"

"Come on over here, out of the wind. See? It's a lot warmer in here." Saying it was warm was stretching the truth a bit, but away from the wind, the rain, and the crashing waves, it actually was. She crouched on a level floor strewn with small rocks and pebbles. Ginette crept in behind her.

Sophie sighed. "So nice and dry in here out of the rain. I wish we had some matches. A campfire would be heavenly."

Ginette nodded. "Yes, campfire. Very nice."

"I bet we'll have one at camp after we get back. This rain can't keep up forever. It has to stop sometime. Let's just rest here for a few minutes."

"Rest. Yes. Rest good," Ginette said. Shivering made her teeth chatter. Even her voice was shaking. She rubbed her arms and hugged her knees.

Sophie leaned back against a round rock, stretched out her legs, and took a deep breath. In the quiet of the cave the sound of the crashing waves was muffled, and she could barely hear the wind in the trees. It was almost cozy.

"You tell me now about Star Girl," Ginette said.

"Well, she's the bravest and strongest person you could ever meet. She's always saving people and catching crooks."

"Save people. That is good," Ginette said, nodding. "You tell me about it."

"In her latest comic a couple of families go on a picnic at a park near a lake one Sunday afternoon. The kids and the parents are having lots of fun playing all kinds of games, but you know something's going to happen. Then, just as they're about to eat their picnic under a giant old maple tree, there's a big earthquake and the tree starts to fall. Star Girl appears from nowhere, with her Star Girl cape flapping in the breeze. She zooms under the tree, pushes it back the other way, and saves all those people from being crushed. Single-handed. And before they can even say thank you, she flies into the sky and disappears."

"I would like to see Star Girl," Ginette said.

"Me, too. She is so brave and so strong. Always helping people. I want to be just like her. I saw a movie about her once. It was so great! Hey, I've got some comics in my suitcase that I'll show you when we get back to camp." She sighed as she remembered. "Another thing I did have was a Star Girl Super Bounce Ball. I sent away for it, and it's so special. Red with a yellow star. But I lost it when we got to camp. Remember when we first arrived and I fell in the water off the boat near the dock?"

"I remember," Ginette said. "But why your ball so special?"

"Well, for one thing, it's a super bouncer. It can bounce as high as a house's roof even. Once I bounced it and it went right onto our roof, so I had to climb up a ladder and rescue it. When I have it in my pocket, it makes me think about Star Girl and how brave and strong she is. And it helps me feel brave and strong, too. You know?"

It was too dark to see if Ginette nodded, but Sophie thought she did. "Your Star Girl ball like my dreidel?"

"Something like that."

"My papa, he very brave all the time. I think he the most brave one, even as brave as your Star Girl, maybe?"

Sophie nodded.

"And he always happy. Singing, make jokes, even when bad soldiers come and we hide under floor. Be like little mice, *comme les petits souris*, he tell us."

"Why did he join the army?"

"When bad soldiers come to our village, he take Maman and baby Selina and me to the country. A farm. Then he go away to fight. But he tell me always be brave and look after Maman and Selina. So we hide in barn for many weeks. No food, just animal food. And we always be so quiet, *juste comme les petits souris*. Like Papa tell us. But one night bad soldiers come and find us, Maman and Selina and me. They march us to concentration camp. Maman go with other ladies, but she tell me be brave and look after Selina, stay with her always. I promise. So I all the time stay with her."

Sophie couldn't begin to imagine the terrible things that had happened to this little girl. She felt so tired that she could hardly keep her eyes open. She sighed deeply and curled into a ball.

Whoosh! Something suddenly whizzed by her face. She gasped, her heart thudding. Then it was gone. High-pitched screeches shot out from the darkness above her head. Giant mosquitoes? Moths? A tiny bird maybe? A second later another flew past her head. Then she knew!

"Bats!" she squealed, leaping up. "This is a bat cave!" She grabbed Ginette's arm and dived out of the cave onto the wet rocks.

"Bats?" Ginette called out to her. "What bats?"

"Souris," Sophie said, trying to remember the French word for *bat*. "It's like *un souris* but has, you know, wings." She flapped her elbows.

"Ooh! *Chauve-souris!*" Ginette squealed, ducking her head and hurrying past Sophie.

Scrambling onto the rocks, they squinted back into the dark cave. Several bats flitted in and out of the opening. Sophie pulled on her hood and tied it tightly under her chin. "Well, that settles it," she said. "Let's get out of here!"

Ginette hesitated, then followed Sophie as they struggled along the cliffs toward the camp. Sophie knew the camp couldn't be that far away, but it was dark and wet and windy and she was exhausted and numb with cold. She felt like curling up right there on the rocks and falling asleep, but she knew they had to keep moving. She didn't dare stop for even a short rest now. If they stopped, she knew they wouldn't be able to get going again.

"Come on, Star Girl, come on," she muttered to herself, forcing one foot in front of the other. "Come on." They stumbled around another point of land that jutted into the sea, and Sophie gaped in disbelief. "Look!" she cried, grasping Ginette's arm. "That's it! That's the dock! Boats! There are the boats! We're here! We made it! Yippee!"

TWELVE

Ginette stared at the camp uncertainly and nervously rubbed her hands together.

"We're going to make it," Sophie said, almost dancing around her. "We will! We just have to get over this next little bit of rocks and we'll be there! We'll be back at camp!"

Ginette crouched on a rock. "No go," she moaned, shaking her head.

"What do you mean, 'no go'? You *have* to go."

Ginette continued shaking her head and moaning, her hands over her ears.

"Look, it's still dark enough that I bet we could sneak right back into our beds and no one will even know we were gone."

Ginette looked up at Sophie, blinking hard. Sophie didn't know what to do. They were so close to camp, and yet Ginette wouldn't move. She was shivering hard.

"It will be so nice and warm in your bunk," Sophie coaxed, patting her arm. "Nice dry warm clothes. Nice warm blankets."

But Ginette still shook her head.

"What are you afraid of?" Sophie asked.

"They come," Ginette mumbled. "They come in night and, and, and..." She looked defeated.

Sophie stood firm. "Not here. No one will come in the night and take you anywhere. I'm your buddy, and I promise nothing bad will happen to you. I'll stick to you like glue every minute. Wherever you go, I'll go. Think of your little sister. You've got to get that dreidel thing to her, remember? And I'll help you do that. I promise."

Ginette continued gazing up at Sophie. "You promise? You promise me?" she whispered.

"Yes, I promise. Cross my heart. Come on. Let's go before we freeze solid to these rocks."

As Sophie climbed up over the last bank of rocks and down into the bay, she turned back. Ginette was moving slowly, but at least she was following her. Sophie breathed a big sigh of relief.

The outlines of the tall flagpole and the buildings under the dark evergreen trees were barely visible. The sky was definitely lighter. It would soon be morning.

"The trick now will be to sneak back into the cabin without waking anyone," Sophie whispered.

But as they slipped and slid down from the mossy rock face into the camp and approached the mess hall along the path, Sophie saw light shining from the big log cabin's windows. Her stomach lurched.

"Maybe it's just Mrs. Carson getting a head start on breakfast," she whispered, hopefully.

As Sophie stepped onto the grassy area near the flagpole, though, the mess hall's door burst open. "There you two are!" Miss Rosy cried, flying toward them.

Sophie swallowed hard. Ginette ducked behind her and clung to the back of her jacket.

Miss Bottomly and Mrs. Carson were on Miss Rosy's heels. They surrounded the girls, hands on hips, faces angry.

"We were about to call your parents!" Miss Rosy said, wringing her hands. "When I woke up and saw that you both were gone, I didn't know what had happened to you. I was at my wit's end! Where on earth have you been?"

Sophie was shivering, and she felt Ginette trembling violently behind her. "It's a long story," she said, putting a protective arm around Ginette's shoulders. "A really, really long story."

"Oh, my!" Mrs. Carson said. "The girls are soaking wet! And they're trembling with cold. Look at the water dripping from their clothes."

"Right," Miss Bottomly said. "Let's get you out of those wet clothes and warmed up right away."

"My oven's already on baking the breakfast buns, so it'll be lovely and warm for you in the kitchen," Mrs. Carson said. She wrapped an arm around Sophie's shoulders and tried to hustle her toward the mess hall door.

Sophie heard Ginette whimper behind her. "It's all right, Ginette," she soothed. "We'll just get warmed up by the stove. It'll be lovely inside."

Miss Rosy gently took Ginette's hand and smiled kindly at her. "Come with me, dear."

Ginette let Miss Rosy lead her into the mess hall.

Sophie had to concentrate to keep upright until she finally collapsed onto a chair in front of the big cook stove. The kitchen was blissfully warm. Her cheeks and hands tingled as the heat melted through the damp cold. The room was lit by two oil lamps, one on a big worktable, and the other suspended from the ceiling near the stove, forming a cozy corner in the dim room. She took a deep breath. The room smelled wonderful, a mixture of fresh baked bread and wood fire. Nothing could smell better.

Miss Bottomly took charge. "Rosy, please go and get something warm and dry for the girls to wear from their suitcases."

When Miss Rosy was gone, Sophie thought with a start, *Oh-oh, my Star Girl comics! She'll find them in my suitcase. Then what? Will she take them away? Tell Miss Bottomly? Will they send me home in disgrace? Can this night get any worse?* She tried to undo the life preserver straps from around her waist, but her numb fingers couldn't undo the knots.

"Let me help you," Miss Bottomly said.

Mrs. Carson was clucking around Ginette. "Your shoes are missing and, look, your poor little toes are all bleeding. I'll get a bucket of warm water for your poor feet and you can take off those wet clothes."

Mrs. Carson looked at Ginette with kindness, but Ginette shook her head and held her sodden jacket closed in a tight fist.

"But you have to get into something dry," Mrs. Carson insisted.

"I change in closet," Ginette said, pulling the large towel out of Mrs. Carson's hands and heading for the broom closet behind the stove. The girl winced as she walked on her bleeding feet.

"Okay, dear. You do that." Mrs. Carson smiled at her. "I'll get some warm water for you, then we'll just wait right here."

Sophie finally got her life preserver off. Then she struggled out of her jacket and peeled off her wet running shoes. Her bare feet were shrivelled and stained blue from the shoes' dye. Miss Bottomly handed her a large towel, which she wrapped around herself after pulling off her clinging wet nightgown. The big towel was scratchy on her bare skin, but it was dry and blissfully warm.

Ginette came out of the closet with the large white towel

draped around her back and arms like an oversize cape. Gingerly she perched on a chair beside Sophie in front of the stove and cautiously put her feet into the pail of warm water Mrs. Carson had placed there for her. She leaned back and sighed. Her pale lips twitched into a small smile.

"Here's a warm drink for you two," Mrs. Carson said, giving them each a steaming mug. "Hot lemon tea with lots of honey."

The hot sweet/sour tea warmed Sophie's insides immediately. She sipped some more and stretched out her tingling feet, resting them on the warm chrome strip at the edge of the wood stove. Sophie wriggled her toes as glorious warmth travelled up her body to meet the warm tea in her stomach. She sighed and closed her eyes. Then Miss Bottomly cleared her throat, and Sophie blinked up at her.

Miss Bottomly was staring down at her, her hands clasped in front of her waist, her dark eyes behind the wire-rimmed glasses questioning, waiting. "Now, girls," she said finally, clearing her throat again, "I want a full explanation. Where have you two been and what in the world were you doing?"

Ginette peered up at Miss Bottomly with big scared eyes, cringing as if she expected Miss Bottomly to start beating her, or worse. She pulled her feet out of the bucket of warm water and retreated into her towel.

"Well, um," Sophie began, glancing at Ginette. How could she tell the whole story and not get Ginette into even more trouble? She decided to just plunge in and try to explain everything as well as she could.

"Some time in the middle of the night I woke up and noticed that Ginette was gone," she started. "She's really worried about her little sister. You see, she can't sleep unless she has her special, um, dreidel. Show her, Ginette." Sophie spoke quickly, hoping the camp leader would see how important this was. "Show Miss Bottomly your dreidel thing."

Ginette fumbled through the folds of the big towel and fished out the wooden top by the long string around her neck. She held it out to Miss Bottomly.

"You see," Sophie went on, "Ginette's little sister can't hear very well and only speaks French. Ginette's the only one who can really understand her, so she wanted to get back to Vancouver right away to find out what's happened to her and make sure the little girl's all right. And she has to give her the dreidel, too."

Miss Bottomly seemed puzzled. "Vancouver?" she said. "That doesn't explain how you two were soaked to the skin and shivering so hard. Start from the very beginning, Sophie."

Sophie glanced at Ginette and thought her buddy nodded, so she took a deep breath and began again. "I woke up in the middle of the night. I guess Ginette woke me up when she came down from the top bunk. I thought she was just going out to the washroom, but when she didn't come back to the cabin, I went to see where she was." And Sophie told them the rest of the story of how she had followed Ginette in the canoe.

"Why on earth didn't you come and get one of the counsellors, Sophie?" Miss Bottomly asked.

"I thought it would be too late. I thought I could catch up to Ginette in the canoe. But is she ever a fast paddler! I paddled really hard, but I couldn't catch up to her at all."

"And where were you going, Ginette?" Miss Bottomly asked.

"I...I go away, um, to Vancouver," Ginette stammered. "*Ma petite soeur...*"

"She has to get to her little sister, Miss Bottomly. You know, to give her the dreidel, and to see that she's okay. She's really worried about her."

"I see," Miss Bottomly said. "You were planning to paddle all the way to Vancouver? Do you have any idea how far that is?"

"First I go to Porteau," Ginette said. "Not so far. We see Porteau from up on the hill yesterday."

Sophie nodded. "On our hike yesterday we looked out over Howe Sound. Miss Rosy showed us where Porteau was, and it really didn't look that far."

"So, Sophie, you eventually caught up with Ginette in another canoe and brought her back?" Miss Bottomly asked.

"Well, not exactly," Sophie said, lowering her eyes. "I wouldn't have caught up with her at all if a big wave hadn't swamped her canoe and sunk it. And then when I managed to paddle to her, my canoe tipped over and we were both in the sea."

"Oh, my heavens!" Miss Bottomly said, her hand covering her mouth. "How did you ever get back to camp?"

"By then we were way too far from the island, so we hung on to the canoe and kicked hard and got to a little islet, just some rocks really. We rested there for a while, then we used a log to help us get back to the island. Then we climbed along the rocks until we finally got back here. It took us forever." Sophie inhaled deeply and let the air out through her nose.

Miss Bottomly shook her head in disbelief. "It's amazing you made it back safely." She narrowed her eyes. "But you should never, ever, have gone out in that canoe on your own. Especially in a storm in the middle of the night."

"I just didn't think there was time to wake you up," Sophie said meekly.

"As for you, young lady..." Miss Bottomly studied Ginette severely.

Ginette's hand shook as she rubbed the dreidel. She frowned with worry, then glanced up at Miss Bottomly with big, frightened eyes.

Sophie remembered her promises to Ginette. She sat up straighter and nudged her chair closer to Ginette's. "I promised Ginette that nothing bad would happen to her. That's the only way she'd agree to come back here."

"Bad?" Miss Bottomly said. "Of course, nothing bad will happen to either of you. That you got back here safely is the main thing. But you must promise never to do such an unwise and dangerous thing again."

"Don't worry," Sophie said. "You have my word on that. I promised Ginette that you'd help her. Can you find out about her little sister, Miss Bottomly? Like, where she is? And can you find out about her aunt, too?"

"I'll make some phone calls later this morning when the rest of the world has woken. Now, let me see those feet of yours, Ginette."

Ginette lifted her feet out of the bucket of warm water. Miss Bottomly tenderly patted them dry and inspected them. "Your cuts don't look too bad."

"Not hurt so much," Ginette said.

"Maybe not now, but they'll be sore later. It's important to keep them clean. Let me bandage them up for you. And here are some clean socks and a pair of running shoes from the lost-and-found that should fit."

After Miss Bottomly gently applied dressings to Ginette's bleeding toes, Ginette carefully pulled on the socks and the white canvas shoes. She nodded up at Miss Bottomly. "Nice shoes," she said. "T'ank you."

Miss Bottomly smiled and patted her head. "You're welcome, dear. Now I imagine that you two would like to go to bed, maybe after a nice hot shower?"

Sophie nodded. "Yes, please."

Miss Rosy arrived with a stack of dry clothes. Sophie held her breath, expecting that she would tell Miss Bottomly about the Star Girl comics, but she didn't say a thing about them. Maybe she hadn't even noticed them in the dark. Fat chance. They were right there under her clothes in her suitcase.

"The girls are ready for a hot shower now," Miss Bottomly told Miss Rosy.

"Righto," the counsellor said cheerfully. "Just follow me, girls."

Sophie tied her towel on a little more securely and slipped on her running shoes. They were wet and cold. She and Ginette followed Miss Rosy along the path to the washroom cabin.

"Should I wait for you?" Miss Rosy asked at the door.

"No," Sophie said. "We'll be okay."

"When you've finished showering, come straight back to the cabin," Miss Rosy said, yawning. "If you don't mind, I don't think I'll wait up for you. I need another hour's sleep before the whole gang wakes up."

The washroom was empty and still lit by the flickering oil lamp. Sophie hung her towel on a peg and turned on the shower. The warm water felt amazing, spraying on her head and streaming down her back. Her skin tingled all over.

"Boy, this feels so great," she said through the cloud of steam. "Come on, Ginette. What are you waiting for?"

Ginette untied her new shoes and pulled off her socks. She hesitated a moment, still clutching her towel tightly around her shoulders. Finally she shook off her towel and hung it beside Sophie's. She stood up straight, held her head high, and stepped into the shower with her eyes closed.

Sophie swallowed a gasp. Long, ugly scars covered Ginette's entire thin body and arms. Angry purple marks disfigured her back and her bottom, and her front, as well. Sophie's heart lurched and pounded and her stomach clenched. What a terrible life that skinny little girl must have had! No wonder she was so scared and mad all the time. Water sprayed into Sophie's eyes. She closed them and turned away.

"Nice," Ginette murmured, water splashing down her scarred back. "Hot water very nice. Very nice."

Sophie tried to smile. She didn't mention the scars. She couldn't even look at them now. She let the warm water beat against her back for a long time until she stopped trembling, until the tears stopped running down her face. Then she turned off the taps.

After drying and pulling on dry shorts, a blouse, socks, and sandals, Sophie blotted her eyes and blew her nose. She followed Ginette back up the trail to cabin four. It was still raining, but not as hard as before. Ginette was limping in her new shoes, but after what she had been through, it was quite amazing that she could walk at all. Sophie thought Ginette must be the bravest person she'd ever known.

Except for the gentle swishing of rain on the roof, the cabin was quiet. No one was stirring. Even Miss Rosy was snoring lightly from behind her screen.

For once Sophie was glad she had the bottom bunk. She didn't think she would have had enough energy left to climb to the upper bunk. She crawled under her blankets without even taking off her sandals and was asleep before her head hit the pillow.

THIRTEEN

It was afternoon when Sophie awakened. A lovely, amazingly sunny afternoon. Sunlight streamed through an open window and hit her face. She blinked her eyes open. The rays felt warm on her cheek. She stretched her arms over her head, rolled out of bed, and glanced into the upper bunk. It was empty.

"I hope Ginette hasn't escaped again," she muttered to herself.

No one else was in the cabin. Mounds of clothes were on the bunks and on the floor. Even Miss Rosy's cubicle behind her screen was untidy.

Sounds of kids screaming and laughing and splashing down by the dock drifted up to the cabin. Sophie skinned out of her clothes and pulled on her bathing suit. It was still damp from yesterday's swim. She shivered slightly as she grabbed her towel and dashed out of the cabin and into the sunshine.

Sunlight was bouncing off the waves in the cove. It looked as if the entire camp was there. Sophie raced down the hill to the flagpole.

The water looked so much friendlier in the sunshine.

"Hey, Soph!" Elizabeth yelled up to her. "Come on in! Water's great!" Even Elizabeth wasn't complaining about getting wet.

Sophie tore down the ramp and leaped off the dock. The shock of the cool water closed over her head and made her gasp, but she soon got used to it. She splashed and kicked though the shallow water in the cove. She was amazed at how good the water felt compared to how cold it had been the night before.

"Hi there, Sophie!" Miss Rosy called out. "Glad you could join us."

Sophie smiled up at her as she swam back to the dock.

"So where have you been?" Elizabeth asked as Sophie pulled herself up onto the dock.

"Slept in," Sophie said.

"So did Ginette. What have you two been up to?"

Ginette was watching Sophie. "I'll tell you later, Liz," Sophie whispered, shaking her head. "Maybe."

"Humph," Elizabeth snorted. "I thought we were supposed to be friends. Why can't you tell me now?"

"Just can't," Sophie said. She knew how much Elizabeth liked to know every last detail about everything.

"Hey, let's all jump in together!" Elizabeth yelled, turning away from her. "All cabin four, up onto the dock," she directed, as bossy as ever.

Sophie followed the other girls from her cabin to the edge of the dock. She stood next to Ginette, who was wearing a bathing suit! The girl also wore the string with the dreidel around her neck and a long-sleeved black shirt that covered her ugly scars. Her toes were plastered with white adhesive bandages.

Ginette actually grinned at Sophie. Then her whole face lit up as she gave Sophie a small red ball with a golden yellow star through it.

Sophie's legs went weak. "My Star Girl Super Bounce Ball!" she cried. "You found it!"

Ginette nodded and smiled wide. She had a space between her two front teeth like Sophie did.

"It stuck under dock there," Ginette said, pointing to the edge of the dock.

"Thank you so much!" Sophie wanted to reach over and hug Ginette hard, but she didn't. She just grinned and jumped around.

"Come on, you guys!" Elizabeth called. "We're all jumping into the water together."

Ginette stood next to Sophie in a line with the other girls at the edge of the dock. Sophie held her Star Girl ball so tightly her fingers cramped.

"Let's say our cheer, then all jump in together at the end," Elizabeth directed. "One, two, three, four. Oh, we're cabin four."

When they got to the "we're rotten to the core" part, they all leaped into the water.

Sophie jumped in, too. Bliss! This was a perfect day! Summer camp had to be the best.

Then the bell clanged, and Miss Bottomly was standing at the flagpole.

"I wonder what's up," Miss Rosy said. "Come on, girls."

Sophie snatched up her towel and followed the other girls trooping up the ramp and gathering around the flagpole.

Miss Bottomly waited until everyone had settled down. "Thank you for gathering so quickly, girls. I have an announcement. It looks like we'll have a beautiful evening tonight, so we'll be able to have our campfire. And we'll have a special talent contest. The winners will receive beautiful gold owl pins like this one, plus a hundred extra points for their cabin."

The girls strained forward to see the gold pin glinting in the sunlight.

"We expect every single one of you to participate in the contest," Miss Bottomly said. "You can tell a story, dance, sing, or do whatever kind of performance you like. In the past we've found that the best ideas are usually group efforts. You'll have the rest of the afternoon to plan and practise. So now I'll leave you in the hands of your able counsellors."

There was a rustling as girls whispered to one another. Excitement filled the air.

As Sophie trailed the girls back to their cabin, she squeezed her Star Girl ball and thought about what she could do for the talent contest. Since her brother, Arthur, was not around to play his harmonica, she couldn't sing. Not all by herself. She would die of embarrassment in front of all those girls.

"Did Miss Bottomly find out about your little sister for you?" Sophie asked Ginette as she caught up with her.

Ginette nodded. "She at special school, boarding school for children who not hear so well. Jericho School? And they understand her talking there. And they give her new dreidel."

"That's wonderful, Ginette. What about your auntie?"

"*Ma tante Lise*, she in hospital. Very good care, Miss Bottomly say."

When Ginette smiled at Sophie, she looked like an entirely different person. Not grouchy or crabby at all. Her blond hair fell in wispy tendrils around her face, and there was even a bit of pink colour in her pale cheeks.

The girls sprawled around the cabin. Elizabeth sat next to Sophie and smiled at her. Sophie smiled back, remembering that she was her friend.

"So what should we do?" Miss Rosy asked them, her pencil poised over her notebook. "Any ideas?"

"What did Miss Bottomly mean by a group effort?" Brenda asked.

"That's when everyone in the cabin does one thing together, like putting on a play," Miss Rosy said.

"That sounds like fun, but we'd have to think of something really interesting," Betty said. "What story could we do?"

Elizabeth twirled around like a ballerina. "I could do a dance from *Swan Lake*," she said. "I know most of it now."

Sophie groaned inwardly as she remembered the talent contest Elizabeth and she had been in last Christmas. Elizabeth could be such a show-off.

"Hmm," Miss Rosy said. "That would take care of one of you."

"Maybe Sophie could do it with me, like a duet. I could show her the steps."

Sophie shook her head. "But I can't dance."

"Maybe Margaret could do it with me then."

"And we could wear silver crowns and be princesses," Margaret said haughtily.

"But what would everyone else do?" Miss Rosy asked.

Ginette was fiddling with the string around her neck. She took out the wooden dreidel and pulled the string from its top, then spun the dreidel on the floor.

"That's an interesting toy, Ginette," Miss Rosy said. "Can I look at it for a sec?"

Ginette reluctantly held it up for Miss Rosy to see, but she wouldn't let it go.

"It's a dreidel," Sophie explained. "It's really special because Ginette's father carved it for her and her little sister. She doesn't want to lose it."

Miss Rosy examined the top more closely.

Elizabeth sniffed. "What's so special about that? Can't he just carve another one for them?"

Sophie shook her head. "He died, you see, in the war. He

fought in the underground resistance movement in France." She looked around the cabin. The girls were all staring at her expectantly. Ginette nodded at her, so she went on with Ginette's story. "He sounds very brave. And Ginette's mother, they haven't found her yet, so Ginette has to look after her little sister now."

"France? Is that where you used to live, Ginette?" Betty asked.

Ginette nodded at Betty. "You tell more," she whispered to Sophie.

Sophie sat up straighter. "Yes. But during the war, she and her little sister had to hide out in the country in a barn with their mom, and they didn't have any food or anything. But some soldiers found them and put them into a place called a concentration camp. The adults and kids were separated, and they lost track of their mom. Even at the end of the war, they couldn't find her. Ginette and her sister were sent to another camp called a refugee camp with a whole lot of other kids until their relatives could be found. And all the time Ginette and her sister stayed together and kept the dreidel."

A hush had fallen over the entire cabin. The girls shook their heads and stared at Ginette and Sophie, riveted. Even Elizabeth and Margaret were mesmerized.

"But how did she come to Canada?" Betty asked.

Sophie glanced at Ginette.

"*Ma tante Lise,*" Ginette said.

"Right, her Aunt Lise," Sophie said. "Ginette and her sister came here with their aunt to live. But she got sick and couldn't look after them, so Ginette's little sister was taken away and Ginette has been really worried about her. She promised her mother and father she would always look after her. But this morning Miss Bottomly found out that Ginette's sister is safe and sound in a boarding school."

"What about the dreidel?" Elizabeth asked.

"Oh, yes, the dreidel," Sophie said. "Her sister needs it to fall asleep. It's like her good-luck charm or a teddy bear. Miss Bottomly said that a woman at the boarding school gave her another one." Sophie gripped her own good-luck charm, her Star Girl ball, tighter.

"So what's going to happen now?" Brenda asked, eyes big with wonder.

"Miss Bottomly is still making some phone calls," Miss Rosy said. "I'm sure we'll get everything sorted out."

"But where will Ginette and her sister live?" Margaret asked. "If they don't have any parents or any other relatives or anything?"

Sophie drew in a quick breath. "I know!" she said. "Ginette could come and live with me and my family for a while. I'm sure Maman and Papa would agree, especially now that my grandmother's gone back to her farm in Manitoba. I have a big room all to myself and Ginette could share it."

"Are you sure, Sophie?" Miss Rosy asked.

Sophie nodded. "Maybe we could ask Miss Bottomly to call my parents. If they say yes, Ginette could come home with me at the end of the week. That is, if Ginette would like that?"

Ginette looked up at Sophie with wide eyes. Then she smiled her gap-toothed smile and nodded eagerly.

Miss Rosy said she would speak to Miss Bottomly.

"I didn't know there were kids that didn't have families left after the war," Elizabeth said. "Nobody told me that."

Margaret shook her head. "I didn't even know there were any kids in the war, period. I thought it was just soldiers fighting."

"Me, too," Peggy said.

"Hey, I just thought of something," Miss Rosy said. "How about we act out the story of Ginette's dreidel for the contest tonight?"

"Yes, let's!" Elizabeth squealed, clapping her hands. "Oh, that'll be really good."

"What do you think, Ginette?" Miss Rosy asked. "Could we use your story to act out tonight?"

Ginette stared at the floor for a moment, then gazed up at Miss Rosy. "I like that."

"Could I be your little sister?" Betty asked her. "I should be because I'm the shortest."

Ginette nodded. The girls gathered around her, and she sat up straighter.

"And I could be your mother," Elizabeth said. "I could do my swan dance for you."

"And I could be your father," Margaret said, lowering her voice to sound like a man. "I'd like to be a soldier for the underground resistance and march around and be brave and everything."

"Okay, okay. Hold your horses. Let's write all this down." Miss Rosy scrambled for her pencil and notebook. "When should we start your story, Ginette?"

Ginette looked thoughtful and fiddled with her dreidel.

Sophie said, "How about when Ginette's dad carved the dreidel and gave it to her and her sister before he left to fight in the underground? What do you think, Ginette?"

Ginette nodded and smiled at her.

"Then we could tell about when the girls and their mother have to hide in the barn, but they're found and arrested and taken to the concentration camp," Miss Rosy suggested.

"Oh, this is going to be so good," Margaret squealed, bouncing on Miss Rosy's bed.

It didn't take them long to get the whole play planned out.

"Let's see," Miss Rosy said. "We'll need a narrator to explain things. How about you be the narrator, Sophie? You definitely know the story best, after Ginette, and you have a good, loud voice."

Sophie agreed, but immediately regretted it. Being the narrator meant she would have to stand in front of the audience the whole time. What if she forgot what she was supposed to say?

"How should we end the story?" Miss Rosy asked. "Any ideas?"

"I think we should sing something," Brenda suggested. "Maybe Ginette could sing? Or maybe Sophie and Ginette?"

Elizabeth nodded. "You should hear Sophie sing. She's got a great voice."

Sophie stared in surprise at Elizabeth.

"Remember when you sang in that talent contest at Sam's Theatre last Christmas?" Elizabeth told her. "You and your brother were great."

"Gosh, thanks," Sophie said, blushing.

"Do you and Ginette know any good songs you could sing for us?" Miss Rosy asked.

Ginette nodded at Sophie and said, "'Au Claire de la lune'?"

Sophie shrugged. "Sure," she told Miss Rosy and the other girls. "We know one that I guess we could start off and the rest of you could join in. It's a song both our dads liked to sing. And it's a song about friends."

"That sounds perfect," Miss Rosy said. "Okay, girls, let's begin. We don't have a lot of time before supper to practise."

The girls all squealed and rushed around.

Supper of hamburgers in big homemade buns, baked potatoes, and corn on the cob dripping with butter was so delicious that, in spite of Sophie's stomach being jittery with nerves, she couldn't get enough. And chocolate brownies and applesauce for dessert was yummy. Sitting across the table from her was Ginette, who certainly gobbled up her share, as well.

Sophie finally understood why Ginette had taken so much food before. They probably didn't have much to eat in the concentration and refugee camps and now she was making up for lost time.

After supper they hurried back to their cabins to prepare a few props for their play and do some last-minute practising.

FOURTEEN

"Fire's burning, fire's burning. Draw nearer, draw nearer." Gentle singing and a strumming guitar wafted in the air from the campfire.

"Okay, troop, time to go," Miss Rosy said. "The show must go on. Break a leg, everyone."

The girls were excited as they filed out of the cabin behind Sophie and Ginette. They took their places on the logs around the campfire and joined in the singing, "Fire's burning, fire's burning."

Sophie's stomach was flip-flopping all over the place. She should never have agreed to be the narrator. Everyone would hate their play. What if she forgot her lines? And she had to sing, too. In front of everyone! They would probably laugh themselves silly at their song. They wouldn't even understand it. If only her brother were here with his harmonica to help keep her in tune.

She gazed at the crackling fire. A log fell and sparks sprayed into the dark. Waves lapped gently on the beach close by. The sky was turning a dark purple that made Sophie think of plums, and one bright star peeped out after another.

"Good evening, girls," Miss Bottomly said when all the girls and their counsellors had assembled on the logs and benches around the fire. "We're all very excited about this talent show. Let's begin right away. Girls from cabin one will start, and cabin two will be next."

"Who'll be the judge?" someone asked.

"So glad you asked," Miss Bottomly said. "The judges will be Mrs. Carson, Mr. Buzz, and me again. We'll be looking at your performances and also watching the audience's reaction. More applause means more marks. So be sure to clap long and hard for your favourite performances."

The girls from cabin one put on a play about Goldilocks and the Three Bears, except they were all campers in a pretend tent with pretend beds. It was pretty funny, but Sophie had to really lean forward to hear Goldilocks. She talked in such a quiet, shy voice.

All during the performances Sophie's nervousness grew. What if Ginette became all grumpy again? She should have told a funny story instead.

She needed some courage, a good boost of courage from Star Girl. She reached into her pocket for her Star Girl Super Bounce Ball. It was round and firm. It was strange that she felt so nervous and scared about a talent show, after what she and Ginette had been through the night before. Ginette didn't seem afraid at all. In fact, she looked all ready to go. Sophie decided that if Ginette could be calm, then so could she. She smiled at Ginette and noticed the girl was clutching her dreidel. Maybe she needed help to be brave, too.

"Now let's hear from the girls from cabin two," Miss Bottomly said.

All the girls from cabin two marched up to the campfire. They were dressed in funny clothes, vests, and paper hats. One of the girls stood forward and announced, "We're going to do a play called 'The Discovery of Gambier Island.' And I'm the narrator."

Everyone clapped politely.

"The year is 1792, over a hundred and fifty years ago. The month is June, and a cold wet June it is. Captain George Vancouver has sailed his ship, the *Discovery*, into English Bay."

One of the campers, wearing a big paper hat and a wooden sword, stepped forward. "Pretty boring around here, mateys. I wonder what lies north. I need six strong and hearty volunteers to come exploring with me."

All the other cabin two campers jumped up and shouted, "Pick me! Pick me!"

"Great!" George said. "The more the merrier. We'll row up the inlet and see what we can see. Don't forget to pack lots of food."

"Maybe we'll find those mountains of gold we heard tell of."

"Early the next morning," the narrator said, "they set out in two rowboats. It's foggy and wet. By afternoon they row past a small island that seems to be in a narrow passage."

"Let's call that Passage Island!" George shouted.

"Righto!" his first mate said, writing on a clipboard with a long feather pen. "Duly noted, sir."

"Before long," the narrator continued, "they spy a large bulbous island with a pointy top."

"Now who does that remind us of?" George asked.

"Ah," the first mate said, "the head of Lord Admiral Bowen?"

"You are correct. Let that island be known henceforth as Bowen Island."

"As they come upon each island," the narrator explained, "Captain George Vancouver names them after different admirals— Bowyer, Keats."

"And that one," George said. "That must be the biggest and lumpiest island of all. A giant haystack with three peaks. Why, it puts me in mind of Lord Admiral Gambier. A large and lumpy man, if I ever knew one. So henceforth this island shall be known as Gambier Island."

The narrator stepped forward and said, "The wind comes up suddenly and blows the small crafts into a bay."

"Heave-ho, my hearties," George said. "Lift your oars. We'll take shelter here. Enough work for one day. Wonder what delicacy the cook will prepare for our supper tonight?"

The narrator said, "And that is how Gambier Island got its name. The end."

All the girls stood in a row and bowed. The audience clapped and cheered.

Sophie thought the cheering was quite loud. She nervously swallowed back a lump in her throat.

"Well done, girls," Miss Bottomly said. "Now it's cabin three's turn."

Miss Bonny stood. "First, we have two people who have jokes to share with you. They're known as the Two Bees."

Beth and Belinda got up and stood in front of the fire. They looked a bit funny because Beth was so short that she had to stand on tiptoe to see everyone in the audience. And Belinda was so tall that she rounded her shoulders to look shorter.

Beth started by saying, "So, Bee One, why did the pig cross the road?"

Belinda shrugged. "I don't know, Bee Two. Why?"

"Because it was the chicken's day off."

The audience laughed, then Belinda said, "Here's a little poem especially for you, Bee Two. 'There are gold ships. There are silver ships. But there's no ship like friendship.'"

"Thanks, Bee One," Beth said. "Okay, I've got a poem for you, too. 'Tell me fast before I faint. Are we friends? Or is we ain't?'"

Then both girls linked arms and said together, "And that's all, folks," and they bowed.

The audience clapped and hooted.

"Thank you, our Two Bees," Miss Bonny said." Next we have Nora and Joan, who have a little song for you."

Nora said, "We thought about this song at suppertime last night, and we'd like to sing it for you."

"And you can join in if you want," Joan added.

"Jelly in the dish, jelly in the dish. Wiggle, waggle, wiggle, waggle. Jelly in the dish. Jelly in the pan, jelly in the pan. Wiggle, waggle, wiggle, waggle. Jelly in the pan." They both sang loudly, wiggling and waggling all around.

The audience loved it. They laughed and clapped and sang along, especially at the wiggle-waggle part.

After a few more acts, Miss Bottomly said, "Thank you very much, cabin three. Let's have the girls from cabin three up here and we'll give them all a good hand."

As the girls bowed to the audience's applause, Sophie eyes were drawn to the horizon beyond the cove where the sky was strangely bright. It was a full moon, rising huge and silent from behind the distant mountains.

"Okay, cabin four," Miss Bottomly said, "your turn next."

Miss Rosy stood in front of all the campers with her back to the campfire. "The girls of cabin four are going to put on a little play for you. And to narrate the play will be Sophie LaGrange. She'll explain everything. Come on up, girls."

Sophie nudged Ginette to stand with their backs to the campfire, which made flickering shadows on the campers' faces.

"Um," Sophie croaked, feeling tongue-tied. She cleared her

throat. Her mouth was sandpaper-dry. For a panicky second she couldn't speak. *All these girls will think our play is the silliest, stupidest play ever,* she thought. *Come on, Star Girl. You can do it. You can!* She squeezed her Star Girl Super Bounce ball in her pocket and pulled in her nervous stomach. Somehow this felt even harder than doing a Star Girl rescue! Even one where she had to follow someone trying to escape in a canoe in the middle of the night.

The audience was quiet and stared up at her, waiting silently with anticipation.

She cleared her throat again and took a deep breath. "This is my buddy, Ginette Berger. And she has something really special. It's called a dreidel." Ginette held up the dreidel and turned left and right so everyone could see it.

Sophie continued. "We're going to tell you the whole story of her dreidel. It's a story that began a few years ago in France when Ginette's father carved it for her and her little sister just before he left to go and fight for the underground resistance movement."

As Sophie told Ginette's story and the other girls acted it out, she forgot about being shy. She looked down at the girls in the audience, and they all stared back at her with shiny and attentive eyes. Miss Rosy nodded at her encouragingly. Sophie's cabin mates acted out their different roles with seriousness and courage, including the part where Elizabeth danced her dance from *Swan Lake,* accompanied by Mr. Buzz on his guitar.

"To finish our story," Sophie said, "we'd like to sing an old French song. It's my dad's favourite, and I just found out that Ginette's father used to sing it, too. It's called 'Au Claire de la Lune,' in English 'By the Light of the Moon.'" Sophie pointed at the round full moon, which hung over the still, dark water and formed a long, glistening path leading all the way into the cove. "The song is about someone named Pierrot who asks to borrow a pen from his friend so he can write a letter. It's a song all about friendship, about old friends and new friends, and about the things we do for our friends. Like Miss Bottomly told us a few days ago, 'A friend in need is a friend indeed.'" She smiled at Ginette, who smiled back, her pale eyes glowing.

Sophie took another deep breath and started to sing. *"Au claire de la lune, mon ami, Pierrot..."* At first her voice came out quiet and trembly, but soon it became stronger and stronger until it was sailing over the dark, swaying treetops. And there was Ginette's voice, too, higher and lighter than hers. Their voices intertwined and soared above the campfire and pierced the night air like long silver arrows.

As Sophie sang, she thought about when she and Ginette were kicking and kicking through that cold night water. Even when the big waves crashed over their heads, they had kept right on kicking and singing at the top of their lungs until they finally made it safely to shore.

For the second verse the other cabin four girls joined in. At the end of the song Sophie bowed low, and so did Ginette and the others.

Except for waves lapping against the rocks and the fire crackling, there was silence. Sophie caught her breath. Then the audience burst into applause. Everyone clapped and hooted. "Bravo! Encore!" they shouted. "Encore!"

Sophie grinned at Ginette and squeezed her hand. Ginette grinned back. All the girls—their friends—held hands and bowed low to the audience again.

At that moment Sophie knew that a friend in need was a friend indeed. In fact, she knew that many friends in need were many friends indeed.

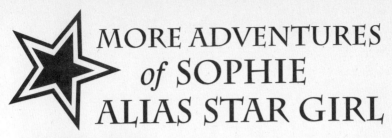

MORE ADVENTURES *of* SOPHIE ALIAS STAR GIRL

SOPHIE SEA TO SEA
NORMA CHARLES

Star Girl is a pint-size superhero with gigantic appeal for ten-year-old Sophie, a French-Canadian girl about to make a cross-Canada move with her family.

In 1949, the year Newfoundland joins Confederation, Sophie soars over flooded prairies, dinosaur badlands, and the peaks of the Rockies. Each chapter/border is a snapshot of provincial history and an adventure in which she flies her cape, and the flag, in the name of Stars everywhere!

YOUNG ADULT FICTION, 8-12
ISBN 0-88878-404-X • 5¼ x 8¼ • 152 PP • $8.95 CDN $5.95 US

CRISS CROSS, DOUBLE CROSS
NORMA CHARLES

Star Girl flies again in this sequel to the best-selling, award-winning *Sophie Sea to Sea*. Starting classes at her new French school in British Columbia, Sophie is happy to escape the old Alderson Avenue School where stuck-up Elizabeth Proctor and her friends rule. But trouble develops when the teachers go on strike and Sophie is forced back into Alderson.

Will she have to endure as an outcast? Or will she, like Star Girl, save the day with a daring rescue?

YOUNG ADULT FICTION, 8-12
ISBN 0-88878-431-7 • 5¼ x 8¼ • 128 PP • $9.95 CDN $6.95 US

 BEACH HOLME PUBLISHING • WWW.BEACHHOLME.BC.CA